Feathered

For Mum, who flew with grace

KCP Fiction is an imprint of Kids Can Press

Text © 2016 Deborah Kerbel

Kids Can Press acknowledges the financial support of the Government of Ontario, through the Ontario Media Development Corporation's Ontario Book Initiative; the Ontario Arts Council; the Canada Council for the Arts; and the Government of Canada, through the CBF, for our publishing activity.

Published in Canada by
Kids Can Press Ltd.
25 Dockside Drive
Toronto, ON M5A 0B5

Published in the U.S. by
Kids Can Press Ltd.
2250 Military Road
Tonawanda, NY 14150

www.kidscanpress.com

Edited by Yasemin Uçar
Designed by Marie Bartholomew
Cover illustration by Simone Shin

This book is smyth sewn casebound.
Manufactured in Shenzhen, China, in 10/2015 by C & C Offset

CM 16 0 9 8 7 6 5 4 3 2 1

Library and Archives Canada Cataloguing in Publication

Kerbel, Deborah, author
    Feathered / Deborah Kerbel.

ISBN 978-1-77138-341-7 (bound)

I. Title.

PS8621.E75F43 2016   jC813'.6   C2015-903360-8

Kids Can Press is a *l*ⓞ*rus*™ Entertainment company

Feathered

DEBORAH KERBEL

 KCP FICTION

PROLOGUE

I'm not crazy. I swear I'm not. Ever since I was old enough to remember, I knew I had it in me to fly. I can't explain it any better than to say it's a feeling so powerful you shut your mouth and don't argue with it.

It's not because of my name. Daddy once said calling me Finch had nothing to do with flying. He said they named me Finch after a character in a famous book. I don't remember which book or which character he was talking about and it's too late to ask now. I guess it doesn't matter, because Mom took me aside afterward and told me that story's not true. She said Daddy hadn't read a book in twenty years and who does he think he's kidding pretending to be some grand reader. She said they named me Finch on account of how I came out of her belly bald and wrinkled and squawking like a baby bird. I guess I believe Mom. She has big honest eyes that can't hide a lie for the life of them.

It's not about my feather either. Although I'm probably the only girl in the whole world to ever grow one. You think I'm pulling your leg, right? Well, I'm not. When I was three years old, Mom plucked a curly white feather out of my neck. How it got there, they couldn't figure. After Dr. Nelson examined me and patched up the back of my neck, he told us to quit worrying. He said the feather probably got stuck in there from me sleeping on top of my quilt instead of under it. Harrison has a different theory. He says I was such a dumb kid, I probably ate my pillow, feathers and all. But I don't think so. Who would want to eat a pillow?

The feather left a little pink scar on the back of my neck. When I get scared or the loneliness comes over me, I run my fingertip over the tiny scar and dream about the day the rest of my feathers will grow in.

That's the day I'll fly away from here.

I might be a clumsy kid on the ground, but in the air I'll be as graceful as a dove.

CHAPTER 1

August 1980

Little House on the Prairie is my favorite TV show ever. I would watch reruns all day if I could. When it's on, it's like my real life falls away and all that's left is Laura Ingalls's world. In my best dreams, I *am* Laura. I call my parents Ma and Pa, wear a sunbonnet wherever I go, skip happily through flower-filled fields and put Nellie Oleson in her place whenever she's nasty. When life gets hard in Laura's world, there's always a nice parent or a kind sister to turn to. Yeah, I think everything was so simple back in those pioneer days. It's like people were so busy churning their own butter and sewing their own clothes, there wasn't time to waste on stupid problems like mine. Back then, you didn't have to worry if you were the only eleven-year-old in your neighborhood who couldn't ride a bike, because back then your family was probably too poor to own a bike anyway. And you didn't have to worry if you were the only kid in class without a pair of Jordache jeans. And nobody laughed if you didn't know how to spell *astronaut* or *telephone* or *vacuum* because those things hadn't even been invented yet! In Laura's world, teachers didn't call their students dumb. And Pa didn't die. Nobody smoked cigarettes until their lungs turned black. And families sat around the table and talked and sang corny songs together every night. If I could beam myself into that TV show, you bet I would.

I hear footsteps overhead and hobble over without my crutches to dial the volume down, in case it's Harrison or his awful friend Matt. Although I'm guessing it's probably just Mom getting up to go to the bathroom. She's changed so much since Daddy died. The old Mom would never have let me sit inside and watch TV on a sunny afternoon in August. The old Mom would have nattered on about "fresh air" and "sunshine" before she shooed me outside, sprained ankle or not. She would have signed me up for day camp, or planned a picnic, or taken me on the bus to the beach or the zoo, or tossed a Frisbee with me. But this Mom doesn't seem to mind if I stay inside. This Mom doesn't say anything when I show up late for dinner. This Mom doesn't pull out the flyswatter when Harrison calls me names at the breakfast table. This Mom doesn't even notice I'm here half the time.

Ever since the funeral last December, she has this empty look in her eyes — like swimming pools drained for the winter. At first, I thought she was mad at Daddy for leaving us. But now I get the feeling she's scared because she doesn't know what to do without him. I haven't told her this, but I'm scared, too. Mom's the smartest person I know, but she's never had a job in her life and she has to go out and get one now. I told her she's smart enough to be a teacher. That sounds like a good job to me. I mean, you get summers off and all. And maybe with a bit of luck, she could teach at my school and take the place of mean old Mrs. Garvin. But Mom says you have to go to a special school for that kind of a job and she doesn't want to start messing around with homework and books and tests all over again at her age.

Teacher school. I think that's kind of funny. I imagine my teachers sitting at a desk like me, doodling on their pencil cases when they ought to be writing down lessons from the blackboard. Can you make a grown-up stand in the corner at teacher school? Or sit in the hall? Or stay for detention? Hey, maybe that's where my teachers learned how to do it to me.

Whenever I suggest a new job idea to Mom, she says we have enough insurance money for now and she'll figure things out if I just quit bugging her about it. Her favorite figuring-out place seems to be the green corduroy chair in the living room. She sits there all day, smoking her cigarettes and staring out the window. Like if she sits and stares for long enough, a job will magically appear. There are days I want to haul her out of that chair and tell her she's never going to figure anything out sitting there all day. But I'm worried that'll make her angry. And something tells me it won't do any good anyway.

When the final credits are over, I flip the channel to see what else is on. A news station is doing a report on Terry Fox. He's the one-legged man with the curly hair who started running across Canada this spring. He's running to raise money so that scientists can find a cure for cancer. On my TV screen, he always looks so small jogging along those big gray stretches of road. I wonder if he's lonely running all by himself. I wonder if I would be. Sometimes when I see his picture, I feel like flying out my front door and never looking back.

Daddy died too soon for Terry Fox's marathon to help him.

The news report ends and suddenly there's nothing left to watch but soap operas and game shows, so I snap off the TV and hobble upstairs for a glass of Kool-Aid. Dr. Nelson said I'm not supposed to be without my crutches for another three weeks, but sometimes I forget them in my room. My room is so messy, it's easy for things to get lost in there. Even something big like a pair of crutches. The old Mom used to harp on me to clean it up. This Mom doesn't say anything about it at all.

When Mom sees me come up the stairs, she waves me over to where she's sitting in the green chair. My heart gives a little jump. "Yes, Ma?" I whisper, leaning down to get a close look at her. Her skin is the color of ashes and she smells of smoke. I push a clump of matted hair away from her face. Her eyes are like fogged-up windows.

"Run to the store and buy me some more cigarettes, would you, Finch?" she says, looking at me but not looking at me. She holds out an empty gold-and-silver package and a five-dollar bill. Her hand is shaking slightly and her fingers are cold as she presses them into my palm. "Show them the package so they'll give you the right one. Okay, honey?"

She shoos me out the door before I can argue.

There's no mention of fresh air or sunshine. And no time to get my crutches.

Laura Ingalls's ma wouldn't do that, I think to myself as I push open the screen door, blinking hard as the sunlight burns my eyes. I pull my imaginary sunbonnet up over my head. And then I pretend I'm Terry Fox as I limp-run down the street to the corner store. The gold-and-silver cigarette package is a crumpled ball in my fist.

CHAPTER 2

The TV set broke today. Right in the middle of the lunchtime news update. One minute a man in a brown three-piece suit was talking about the hostages in Iran and the next minute there was a loud pop and the screen became a fuzzy wall of gray. A weird burning smell came spewing out from behind the TV set, so I grabbed my crutches and limped out of there fast, just in case the whole thing decided to blow up. In the end, that didn't happen. But I went to make myself a snack before breaking the news to Mom.

I think about those poor hostages a lot. It's coming up to a year now since they were captured. Can you imagine not being able to go outside for a whole year? I can't. And how can they go that long without changing their underwear? I asked Harrison about it once, but he gave me that look that said, Quit bugging me with your stupid questions. So I shut up and didn't ask again.

My stomach lets out a soft growl as I limp into the kitchen. The word *hostages* always makes me think of the word *sausages*. Is that bad? And then I'm thinking about the big Sunday breakfasts Daddy used to make, and a giant bubble of loneliness swells inside me. Pulling open the snack cupboard, I run my fingers over my feather scar and stuff a Fudgee-O into my mouth to make the feeling go away.

When I'm done eating, I head to the living room to check on Mom and see if she's figured anything out yet. But my feet freeze on the edge of the brown shag carpet. Harrison's long legs are sprawled over the couch and he's showing off his Rubik's Cube skills to awful Matt. The way my brother's fingers spin and twirl over the bright colors of that cube is hypnotic. He makes it look so easy, even though I know for a fact it's not. I can't even get three rows to match up, but my brother can get them all. Luckily, Matt's too busy watching Harrison solve the cube to notice me. I back up and sneak out of the house before that changes, bringing the screen door closed behind me with a soft click. I don't want another body part to get sprained today, thank you very much. And when Matt's nearby, you never know what sort of bad things might happen.

It was only three weeks ago when I had to jump

out my window to get away from him (which is how I hurt my ankle). I was watching TV when he snuck up behind me, silent as a snake. I felt something soft and fuzzy sliding up the back of my arm and turned around with a start. There was awful Matt, holding up a dead mouse by the tail and grinning at me with his goat face and his crooked yellow-toothed smile. "Brought you a present, Flinch," he said, swinging the poor thing back and forth like a yo-yo, bringing the furry corpse closer to my face each time. You can bet I screamed so loud, my throat hurt for days after. Then I jumped up and started to run. Matt chased me, of course. The one time I dared to look behind me, he was on my heels, his eyes glittering with danger. His legs are so much longer than mine, I only got as far as my bedroom before he caught up.

"Kiss the rat, Flinch," he said, grabbing my arm and pushing the mouse in my face. "Kiss it and I'll let you go."

My body had switched to full panic mode. Somehow I found the courage to kick him in the shins and yank my arm away. My eyes did a quick scan of the room. As far as I could see, there was only one escape route. And I was positive it wouldn't fail me. I was born to fly, after all.

I scrambled up onto my window ledge and pushed

out the screen. Running a finger over my scar, I made a wish that the rest of my feathers would come right now. This was the moment I needed them most. "Finch, don't!" I heard Harrison yell from somewhere in the distance as I hurled myself into the air.

I remember the smooth feel of the wind rushing over my face and my arms. I closed my eyes, and for a split second I was sure I had done it. I was flying. A second later the ground rose up to meet me with a powerful smash. The boys found me a few minutes later on the grass outside. "You little moron. Get up before Mom finds out," Harrison snarled, hooking his hands under my pits and pulling me to my feet. My ankle roared with pain and I passed out cold in his arms. But not before I heard Matt hissing his signature warning over my ear: "Better not tell."

And of course, I didn't. Who would I tell anyway? For sure not Mom. The way she's been acting lately, I don't even know if she'd hear me. Harrison knew the truth, but he wasn't about to defend me against Matt, that's for sure. Matt's pretty much his only friend these days. He's not going to give that up, even for the sake of his little sister's safety.

Harrison wasn't always mean to me. For most of our lives, we were really close. It's only in the past year that he's turned sour. Like a carton of milk that's been left in the fridge past its expiration date. I think some of it has to do with losing Daddy. But I think most of it has to do with awful Matt.

Whenever that boy's around, every part of me feels sprained.

In the end, I told Mom and Dr. Nelson that I hurt my ankle falling down the stairs. Mom didn't question it. I've always been a clumsy kid, so falling down a flight of stairs wouldn't be out of the ordinary for me.

I head to the backyard, hoping Harrison and Matt won't find me there. On my way around the side garden, I glance at the house next door and catch a quick glimpse of a little girl's face in the window. Our eyes connect for the tiniest second before she ducks out of sight. I wait a moment to see if she'll come back to the window, but she doesn't. She's one of two girls who moved in with their parents just last month. Except for moving day, we haven't seen much of them. Usually it's just the father coming and going in his navy blue suit and his white Chevrolet. Sometimes the daughters run out to the driveway to greet him or to kiss him goodbye. But then they always disappear right back into the house again. At first when I heard a family with two little girls was moving in, I was so happy. The previous owners were an old couple who didn't like children, as far as I could tell. Since the minute the moving vans drove away, I've been dying to go knock on the door and say hello. But Mom won't let me. "Don't be a pest, Finch. Give the poor family some time to get settled in," she said.

You can bet the old Mom would have brought them a casserole on their first day here. Laura Ingalls's ma would have, too.

Harrison said him and Matt saw the girls last week, climbing into the car with their parents. He told me Matt said the mother's clothes looked funny, like she was wearing pajamas, and that he called them a bad word that makes me hate him even more than I already did. I wish they would come out to play one of these days.

When I get to the backyard, I pull out my green Frisbee and practice my throw. Daddy bought it for me last year. He said catching a Frisbee was less tricky than catching a ball. He was right. I love tossing it and watching it float through the air like a mini UFO. On the fifth throw, the Frisbee lands under my favorite tree — the big, spreading chestnut that takes up the entire south side of the backyard. When I bend to pick it up, a soft chirping noise catches my attention. There's a baby bird lying on the grass. Its eyes are closed and its pink featherless body is flailing like a drowning victim. I look up and spot the nest perched on a low-hanging branch. "Did you fall?" I ask, reaching down to pick it up. I cup the little bird in my palm. Its squiggly body feels cool against my skin. I hold it a minute to warm it, then reach up and carefully put it back in the nest with its brothers and sisters. There are four baby birds altogether, each one as naked and fragile as the next. After that, I make sure to throw my Frisbee on the other side of the yard. Just to be safe.

At dinner, I confess to Mom about the broken TV. "The picture just disappeared. It wasn't my fault. Honest, I didn't do anything." She blinks and sighs.

"I'll call a handyman tomorrow," she mumbles. But I know what she's thinking, 'cause I'm thinking the same thing. If Daddy was here, he'd have taken care of it. We never needed a handyman before he died.

I push my food in circles around my plate. Fish sticks and ketchup. Mom's made the exact same dinner for three weeks straight. I'd complain about it if I thought it would do any good. The strange part is, she's a really great cook. When Daddy was alive, she made sure we sat down together for dinner every night. A big homemade dinner with each and every food group properly represented. And she always loved making up new recipes and trying them out on us. Nowadays, it's either frozen food or takeout. It's gotten so bad, Harrison usually doesn't bother coming home to eat anymore. He eats at Matt's house now and, as much as I hate Matt, I can't say I blame him, 'cause dinners around here are as much fun as getting a tooth drilled. It's probably one of the reasons my brother puts up with Matt — just so he can get a decent meal once in a while. Every night at dinner, Mom sits with her chair angled toward the window, sipping from a glass of water and puffing on those awful cigarettes. As far as I can tell, she never eats anything anymore. I don't think I've seen her put a crumb of food in her mouth since Daddy's funeral.

I just hope those cigarettes of hers are packed with vitamins and minerals … like the commercial says for my Apple Jacks.

CHAPTER 3

Matt and Harrison are hanging out at our house again today. Which means I'm hiding out in the backyard. I don't mind so much. Our house is built on the edge of a small forest that borders a ravine. Between catching water striders, climbing trees and making daisy chains, there are lots of "pioneer girl" things for me to do to pass the time. The first thing I do is check on the birds' nest. Their tiny twig home is so perfect and round ... like a beautiful work of art. I'm relieved to see the baby birds are all still there. When I chirp a hello, they stick their little yellow beaks up in the air and squawk. They must be hungry, poor things.

"Don't worry, guys," I whisper, "I bet your mom is coming with food soon."

I decide to leave the pioneer girl stuff for later and work on my Frisbee skills for a while. But after about half an hour of practicing the perfect toss, I watch it sail onto the next-door neighbor's back porch. I stare at it for a minute while I consider my options.

1. Leave it and go play something else.
2. Hobble into their backyard and use my crutch to knock it off their porch.
3. Go ring the doorbell and ask for it back.

It's an easy choice. They've had a month to settle in, after all.

Their doorbell gongs like organ chimes. After a minute or two, the knob turns and the door opens with a creak. A small girl with brown skin and long black hair appears in front of me. Her hair is parted in the middle and held back neatly with a pair of red barrettes and matching ribbons.

"Hello?" She says it like she's asking a question. Her big eyes glide over me suspiciously. I smile and give her a little wave.

"Hi, I'm Finch. I live next door."

She cocks her head, like she's trying to figure out why I'm here. An even smaller girl pokes out from behind her. She's sucking her thumb so hard, it squeaks.

"My Frisbee landed on your back porch," I say. "I came to get it."

The girl's shoulders relax. For some reason, she

seems relieved to hear this. "What happened to you?" she asks, pointing to my crutches.

"Oh. I ... um, fell down the stairs."

She nods but doesn't say anything.

"So, is it all right if I come in so I can get my Frisbee?"

She glances behind her, like she's checking for permission. "Okay, quickly," she whispers, waving me in. Silently, we walk through the cool air-conditioned house toward the back door. I've never been inside this house before, so I'm surprised to see it's the exact same layout as ours. Except everything's flipped the opposite way ... like it's a *Through the Looking Glass* version of my own house. I'm guessing this new family's furniture must not have arrived yet, because except for a couple of chairs and a few floor pillows, the house is completely bare. We pass behind a thin woman who's kneeling on the hardwood floor in front of a shiny golden statue. The statue is wearing a garland of yellow and pink flowers. The woman is wearing a flowing orange shirt and matching pants. A tidy black braid hangs down the length of her back.

The girl holds a finger up to her lips. "Mother's praying," she says softly. The woman seems to be talking to the statue. As she raises her hands to her face, her collection of gold bracelets fall to her elbow. They jingle like little bells. I want to ask the girl what her mother's praying for, but I stop myself. I'm smart enough to understand that I should be quiet when someone is praying. Kind of like how I imagine people would act at church. The girl leads me through the house to the sliding glass doors at the back. The little sister trails behind us like a tiny shadow. When we get to the back porch, the older girl picks up my Frisbee from the deck floor and hands it back to me. I can tell she's pleased with herself for helping. We make our way back to the front door, quiet as ghosts.

"Thanks," I say, once I'm sure we're far enough away not to disturb her praying mom. "Do you want to come outside and play with me?"

"I don't know," she replies, twirling a strand of glossy hair around and around her finger. "I'll ask Mother later."

"We could play catch with my Frisbee. And I've got a badminton set in my backyard. And croquet, too."

She stares at me like I'm speaking a foreign language. "My name is Pinky Nanda," she finally says. "This is my sister, Padma."

Padma is holding on to her big sister's leg like her life depends on it.

"Nice to meet you," I say, sticking out my hand.

After a second, Pinky reaches out to shake it. A gold bracelet circles her wrist ... a perfect match for the little gold hoops in her ears. I wonder if her family is rich. No kid I know wears real jewelry like that. "You're pretty," I say. She smiles a shy smile. "How old are you?" I ask.

"Eleven."

I'm surprised to hear she's my age. She looks so much smaller than me.

"How do you like your new house?"

She shrugs. "I like it. But I liked our old house more. It was next to a park ... and I had a bigger room."

"So why did you move?"

Another shrug. "My father said it would be better here," she says. Then she presses her lips together like she's trying to stop something else from coming out.

Better than what? I can't help wondering.

"You're coming to school in September, right? We'll be in the same grade. Maybe the same class."

She glances around again. Like she's worried someone might be listening. "I hope so." She says it so softly it's barely a breath. "But I have to see what my father says. He might sign me up for a different school."

This surprises me, too. "Why? Roseborough's the closest. You can walk there in ten minutes."

"He thinks a Hindu school is ... better. He says I'll like the kids there more. And learn more important things. But Mother doesn't think so."

"Well, they better decide fast because my school starts in two weeks," I say. "The day after Labor Day. Just cross your fingers you don't get Mrs. Garvin. I had her last year. She's horrible."

Pinky chews on her lip and doesn't reply. Suddenly, I hear her mother calling from the other room. Her words sound fast and bubbly — like spilled marbles rolling across the floor. Pinky answers quickly, then turns back to me and pulls open the front door. "You have to go now." She places a hand on my shoulder and presses me through the doorway. "Bye-bye."

"Let me know about school, okay? We can walk together if you want. But your parents have to register you with the office ..."

Behind me, the door closes with a click. I stare down at the Frisbee in my hands, wondering what on earth I did wrong.

Harrison and Matt are in the backyard when I return with the Frisbee. Too bad I'm not quick enough on my crutches to escape.

"Hey — you still crippled?" Matt says, running to cut me off before I can get away. He grabs one of my crutches and tosses it to Harrison. "Thanks. We've been looking for a baseball bat. Right, Harr?"

I turn to look at my brother, pleading silently with him to give it back. The last thing I want to do is give Matt the satisfaction of hearing me beg. But Harrison doesn't make a move. He just stares at the ground like I'm not even there. Before I know what's happening, Matt karate chops the other crutch out from under my arm. Now I'm standing there on one foot, feeling like a snail without a shell.

"You didn't tell anyone about our game of Kiss the Rat, did you?" he says, stepping closer. His breath smells like rotten eggs. I put a hand over my nose and shake my head. "Good," he says. He leans toward me and yanks the top edge of my yellow tube top back with his dirty-nailed fingers. He takes a second to steal a look at my skinny bare chest before letting it snap closed. My face burns with embarrassment. I clutch my top to myself, too scared and ashamed to make a sound. He smirks and picks my karate-chopped crutch off the ground. "Cool it, Flinch. It's not like you have anything worth looking at anyway."

Now my cheeks feel like someone's lit them on fire.

"Hey, Matt! Look what I found!" Harrison shouts from the other end of the yard.

He points up into the chestnut tree. My heart stops.

"No!" I screech. But Matt's already bounding across the grass like a German shepherd unleashed. Before I know what's happening, he lifts my crutch in the air and topples the bird nest from the branch. I can hear the little babies chirping in distress. He bends down and picks up the nest. The birds are still inside. I can see their bright yellow beaks from here.

Then he picks up one of my badminton rackets from the grass at his feet.

Stop! I want to scream. *Leave them alone!* But I can't say anything at all. Someone's poured cement down my throat.

"Cut it out, Matt," I hear Harrison say. But he's too late.

"Keep your eye on the birdie, Flinch!" Matt hollers, tossing the little twig nest in the air and whacking it so hard it explodes on contact.

I scream and sink to my knees in the soft grass, squeezing my eyes shut so I don't have to see anymore. Then I cover my face with my hands so that awful Matt won't know how hard he's made me cry.

CHAPTER 4

Mom didn't get out of bed this morning. When I go to check on her, she's lying on her side with the covers pulled up over her ear. But she isn't asleep. Her blue eyes are wide open and staring at the wall.

"Ma?" I whisper. She doesn't answer. I wonder if maybe she's coming down with a cold or flu. Or worse, a case of scarlet fever. In *Little House on the Prairie*, that's what made Laura's sister Mary go blind. Or maybe she caught cancer, like Daddy and Terry Fox did. I'm scared now, so I walk over to her bedside and put my hand on her forehead, just like she does for me when I'm sick. No fever. Her skin is as cool as cucumber soup.

"I'm fine, Finch. I just don't feel like getting up yet," she mumbles when I ask what's wrong. I lean down to kiss her tousled hair. Her eyes flutter closed. I linger in the doorway for a few minutes, wondering what to do next. My stomach growls loudly.

In the kitchen, I get myself a bowl and a spoon, a

carton of milk and a near-empty box of Apple Jacks. I mix it all together and, voilà ... breakfast is served. Harrison's not home, so I sit at the table by myself. I don't care, though. I'm still so angry at him for letting Matt smash the birds' nest, I've vowed to never speak to him again.

After washing up my bowl and spoon, I check on Mom again, but this time she's fast asleep and snoring softly. I feel weird and alone. Except for the hum from the window air conditioner, the house is as quiet as night. Like I'm the only person awake in the world. I slip on my shoes, go outside and sit in the shade of the house by the side garden. I don't want to go into the backyard again. Not after what Matt did.

The sun is shining and the sky is as blue as Mom's favorite eye shadow. The one she used to wear when her and Daddy would go out to a restaurant for dinner and leave Harrison and me with a crummy babysitter. Mom doesn't wear eye shadow these days. Or lipstick or blusher either.

I pick a flat blade of grass, stretch it between my thumbs and make whistling sounds. I consider ringing Pinky's doorbell again and asking her to come outside and grass-whistle with me. But a moment later, I see her face pop up in the window across from where I'm sitting. I drop the blade of grass and wave eagerly. She ducks away. I wait to see if she'll come back, but she doesn't, so I walk over to the window and peer inside. I can see the Nandas' kitchen — the mirror image of ours. Except their version is all neat and tidy with no dirty ashtrays or stacks of dishes cluttering the counters like in my house. There's a folded newspaper sitting at the edge of the wooden table and an empty teacup and saucer beside it. On the wall facing me, I spot a painting of an elephant sitting cross-legged on top of a giant flower. The elephant is dressed in bright clothes and it's wearing jewels and a pink-and-yellow garland that reminds me of the one on the golden statue Mrs. Nanda was praying to the other day. At the elephant's feet is a tiny mouse nibbling on a piece of food. I think it's probably the strangest painting I've ever seen. I scan the room for Pinky but can't see her anywhere. So I knock softly on the window.

"Hello?" I say, even though I don't know if she can hear me through the glass. I wait a minute and knock again. "Pinky? Are you there?" Still nothing. I wait another minute. Just as I'm about to give up, Pinky's face slowly rises from beneath the window, where I realize she must have been hiding all this time. Her eyes are big and skittish. Her mouth is puckered tight like a silent kiss.

I jump with surprise. "Oh, hi!" I shout, excited to see her. She quickly holds a finger up to her lips and points another finger over her shoulder. Without saying a word, I understand that I'm supposed to be quiet, although I'm not really sure why. Maybe her mother's praying again? I nod to let her know I get it. "Come out and play," I whisper, pointing at her and then gesturing behind me in the general direction of outside. She shakes her head to say no, and I'm disappointed but I guess not really surprised. Even though I still don't get why her and her sister always stay inside. I frown really hard so she'll understand that I'm sad that she can't come. She sad-faces me back and then wipes pretend tears away from her eyes. I smile at that. I want to keep our conversation going so I throw my hands over my eyes, tilt my head back and pretend to wail like a baby. When I look back at Pinky, she's laughing. I can even hear her bouncy giggle through the window. I laugh, too, and point to her as if to say, "Your turn now," and suddenly it turns into a game of Who Can Make the Silliest Face? We go back and forth for a few minutes and I think it's the most fun I've had in a long time. I cross my eyes and make moose ears. She sticks her tongue out so far, it touches her nose. I make bunny teeth and a pig nose. She sucks her cheeks in so deep, it looks like her face is folding in half. Then out of the blue, Pinky's silly face disappears and her body stiffens. Now she's turning and running out of the kitchen without even a wave goodbye. I wait a long time to see if she'll come back and continue our game. But she doesn't. I decide to go back inside.

By lunchtime, Mom's still not out of bed. I make myself another bowl of cereal and wonder if I should call Dr. Nelson. I decide to wait a little bit longer. The sound of my chewing is deafening. The doorbell rings halfway through my cereal. It's Detective Kroon — Daddy's best friend from school.

"Hey, Finchie," he says, leaning his broad shoulder against the door frame. "I was in the neighborhood and thought I'd stop by to see how everyone's doing? Is your mom here?"

"She's not feeling well," I say quietly.

"That's too bad. A cold, is it?"

I'm not sure how to answer that question because I honestly don't know what's wrong with Mom. Maybe I should ask him to come in and feel her forehead for me. Maybe he'll know why she doesn't feel like getting out of bed today. But if he wakes her up, Mom might be mad. So I just shrug.

He scratches his chin. "What about your brother? Is he home?"

I shake my head. "He's out."

Detective Kroon watches my face carefully, like he thinks maybe there's something more I might want to tell him. "Your daddy asked me to watch out for you guys. Did you know that, Finchie?" His voice is very serious now.

"Yes."

"And you know that I told him I would, right?"

I nod.

"So if there's ever anything I can help with ... or anything you need, you just have to say the word. Okay?"

I nod again. I always liked Detective Kroon. He used to give me piggybacks and airplane rides. I wonder if I should tell him about the empty look in Mom's eyes. Or the cigarettes she smokes all day. Could he help make those things go away? What about awful Matt? Could he arrest him for killing those poor baby birds? I shuffle my feet, wondering what I should say and what I shouldn't. But before I can figure it out, the radio on Detective Kroon's belt goes off. A staticky voice squawks his name. He holds it up to his ear and frowns.

"Darn. I gotta go," he says, pulling his car keys out of his pocket. "But call me if there's anything you need. And be sure to tell your mom I hope she's feeling better soon, okay?"

With a wink and a wave, he's gone. I go back to the kitchen and eat my soggy Apple Jacks. Just before one o'clock, Mom finally gets up. She staggers to her figuring-out chair and pushes a cigarette into her mouth. Her eyes look red, like she's been crying.

"Sorry, Finch. It must have been one of those twelve-hour bugs that are going around," she says. The cigarette between her lips bobs up and down with each word. For once I don't feel like pulling it out of her mouth. I'm just happy she's awake.

"Detective Kroon came by while you were sleeping. He said to say hi and that he hopes you feel better."

Mom looks surprised at this. Her forehead crinkles. "What did you tell him?"

The way she says it makes me wonder if I did something wrong. "I ... I just said you weren't feeling well." Then I add, "He wanted to see how we were doing. He said Daddy asked him to watch out for us."

Mom's cheeks go pink and she runs her fingers through her messy hair like a makeshift comb. "You really shouldn't be telling people my business, honey," she says, flicking the little wheel of her blue lighter. She does this several times before a flame appears. "It looks like a beautiful day. Why don't you go outside and get some fresh air?"

This sounds so much like my old mom that I want to throw myself into her lap and cry with relief. Then she lights that cigarette and turns to stare out the window. The empty look falls over her eyes. And the moment's gone.

Through the window, I can see the giant chestnut tree in the backyard; its leaves are shivering in the breeze. My brain starts to think about those poor baby birds, but it's just too sad, so I make it stop. I think instead about the broken TV downstairs. I wonder if the hostages have been freed yet. I wonder where Terry Fox is running today. I wonder which *Little House on the Prairie* episode I'm missing. I'll be upset if it's the one where Laura puts apples down her dress.

"Did you call a handyman, Ma?"

The tip of her cigarette glows orange. Then smoke curls out from her nostrils, like a dragon's fiery breath. "I'll do it later," she says. "And why are you calling me 'Ma'?"

I reach for my crutches. "I'm going outside now."

Since the TV's still broken, I take some money from my piggy bank and walk up the street to the movie theater. I buy a ticket for a movie starring the same blonde actress from *Grease* and find a seat by myself in the last row. I think about school while I wait for the movie to start. I wish I never had to go back. Every year, my teachers say the same things about my writing and spelling.

"Pay attention."

"It's not rocket science."

"Just do it."

"Neater, Finch — don't be lazy."

I'm pretty good at reading, but writing is different. My hands never want to do what they're supposed to do. Some of my teachers have tried to be nice about my writing. But the worst teachers are the ones who make me feel like it's my fault. Every year since I can remember, Mom goes to the school to talk to my teachers about my writing. And, until Daddy died, she did what she could to help me with my homework. But, as smart as Mom is, even she doesn't understand why I can't get the work done the way the teachers want it. When Daddy was alive, he'd sit with me and help me with my numbers and letters on weekends when he wasn't working. He told me school never came easy for him either.

Maybe that's why him and I got along so well.

Last year was the worst. If there were awards for

the meanest teacher in the world, Mrs. Garvin would have won the top prize — no contest. She must have learned some bad lessons at teacher school, 'cause for some reason I never understood, she was only nice to the kids who were popular or smart. She called me slow and lazy and warned me I was going to have to repeat the year if I didn't smarten up. She did it so much, after a few months the rest of the kids in my class started calling me slow and lazy, too. Somehow I managed to squeak through the year with a passing grade. But it's safe to say I hate school almost as much as I hate Matt. And that's saying a lot.

I decide not to get up when the movie ends. When the usher comes by and asks me to exit the theater, I point to my crutches, let out a fake moan and tell him I'm too hurt to move. He frowns at me but doesn't argue. I sit there while they roll the movie again. By the time I get up and go home for dinner, I know some of the songs by heart.

And I'm so hungry, even fish sticks and ketchup sound good.

CHAPTER 5

September 1980

I spend most of the night before the first day of school tossing back and forth under my quilt and worrying about sixth grade. I really hope this year is better than the last one. It has to be.

In the morning, I hang around on the sidewalk outside my house for a few minutes, waiting to see if Pinky will come out and walk with me. But she doesn't come and I end up walking to school alone. I get there just in time for the first bell, which shrieks through my ears like a siren. The first thing we're supposed to do is go to the gymnasium for a morning assembly, where they're going to announce our teachers for the year. I push my way into the crowd, all of us trying to squeeze through the narrow doors at the same time. Lucky for me, Dr. Nelson gave me the okay to stop using my crutches just in time for the first day of school, which was a relief 'cause I sure don't need another reason to stick out like a sore thumb around this place. I spot Harrison and Matt on the other side of the gym, but neither of them sees me. I grab a spot on the floor, hug my knees to my chest and keep an eye open for Pinky. But I don't see her anywhere. Maybe she's late. Or maybe her parents haven't gotten around to registering her yet. Or maybe they're sending her to a Hindu school, after all. I think about Pinky's wide eyes staring out at me from behind the silver window. And the little golden statue in her living room. I try to imagine what her mother would have been praying for that day. I've never once seen Mom pray. Not even when Daddy was sick.

Karen Simons sits down in front of me. She lives on my street and, up until last year, used to be my best friend. I stare at the back of her T-shirt and think about all the times we used to play together. When we were six, I taught her how to turn a somersault. When we were seven, she taught me how to French braid my hair. I gave her a Barbie doll for her eighth birthday. She gave me a record for my ninth. I was the first person she told when her parents divorced last summer. She was the first person I told about Daddy getting cancer. Then last spring, she up and decided our friendship was over.

Just like that, she started caring about clothes and boys and ignoring me. When I asked her why she wouldn't talk to me anymore, she said, "Get off my case, toilet face." Now Shawna Frankel is her best friend. The two of them share clothes and secrets and get their hair cut in the exact same style. If you saw them from behind, most likely you wouldn't be able to tell them apart.

Our principal, Mrs. Fiorini, walks to the center of the stage and taps the microphone. Once we're all quiet, she starts reading off the class lists in a monotone voice that sounds like one of those robot recordings. She starts with the youngest grades and slowly works her way up. An itchy heat breaks out over my skin while I wait for her to get to the sixth graders and I actually have to sit on my hands to keep from scratching my arms and legs raw. There are going to be two sixth-grade classes this year. One of them is being taught by horrible Mrs. Garvin and the other one's being taught by a young teacher with feathered red hair who Harrison had when he was my age. I don't remember her name right now, but Harrison always said she was really nice. You can bet I'm hoping to get in that class. In front of me, Karen flicks her perfectly brushed hair. She turns slightly and catches my eye but quickly looks away like she doesn't see me. Then she leans over and whispers something in Shawna's ear and they both giggle. A minute later, Mrs. Fiorini starts reading off the sixth-grade class lists. I hear Mrs. Garvin's name called. And then I hear my name called. And then I don't hear anything else 'cause the gymnasium ceiling comes crashing down over my head.

Not really. But it feels that way.

How is it possible that I'm in *her* class again? How am I going to survive another year like the last one? I have to bite my lip to keep from crying right there in the middle of the assembly. I bite it so hard, I taste blood. Lowering my head, I tuck my face into my knees until Mrs. Fiorini stops talking. When it's time to leave, I take a deep breath and lift my head, staring in surprise when I see Karen stand to go. Her lime-green T-shirt is stretched over her brand-new bumps. And she's wearing a pair of Jordache jeans that are so tight, you could count the change in her pocket. What happened to her this summer? It looks like she transformed into a totally different person in just two months. She's even wearing pink lip gloss. So is Shawna.

Suddenly I feel like running out the gymnasium doors and not stopping until I'm far, far away from this school. If I had my feathers I'd fly away — fly until my arms give out ... or until there's no sky left. But I don't. Instead, I pick myself up off the floor and walk out of the gym, following Karen and Shawna up the stairs to Mrs. Garvin's class. When I get there, I take a seat at the very back of the room. With any luck, maybe she won't notice me till next June.

Too bad for me, I have no such luck. Right after attendance, Mrs. Garvin makes us write a paragraph about "What I Did Last Summer." It's exactly the same thing she made us do on the first day of fifth grade, which makes me feel déjà vu—ish in a really bad way. Within seconds, the air around me fills with the sounds of pencils scratching paper. I pull a freshly sharpened #2 pencil out of my schoolbag and stare down at the blank notebook page in front of me.

This isn't going to turn out well. I know this for a fact.

But there's absolutely no escaping it. This is also a fact.

I adjust my pencil grip while I try to remember all the advice Daddy used to give me.

Take your time, Finch ... Don't worry about the spelling ... Just get your ideas out. That's what matters most.

Mrs. Garvin is walking up and down the aisles between the desks, reading over everyone's shoulders. My hand starts to quiver as I slowly push my pencil across the page.

This summer I wached Terry Fox running on tv.
He is tryng to help find a cuer for canser.

Don't rush, Finch, Daddy's voice calmly reassures me. *Take all the time you need ... It's okay if it doesn't look perfect ... You can do it.*

"Five more minutes, people," Mrs. Garvin warns.

I think he is reely brave. I hope i can do sumthing brave like Terry Fox won day. maybe I can —

Mrs. Garvin's brown penny loafers pause beside my chair. My pencil freezes mid-sentence. "Sit up straight, please," she says, tapping her twelve-inch ruler against the top of my desk. Her eyes float over my page and she lets out a tired-sounding sigh. "I see nothing's changed with you over the summer, Miss Bennett."

"You can say that again." Karen giggles from two rows up.

I feel my face go warm.

Mrs. Garvin waves her hand over my paper but doesn't touch it. Like she'll get cooties if she touches it. "This is unacceptable," she says, clucking her tongue. "An absolute embarrassment."

"Just like her mother," Karen whispers to Shawna, covering her mouth with her hand. Now my face is boiling hot. I think about the time two summers ago when Karen fell down on her roller skates outside my house and I practically carried her inside and patched up her shredded knees all by myself 'cause there wasn't a grown-up around to help. I think about all the times Mom would invite her to stay for dinner and make a special dish just for her because she's picky and didn't like what the rest of us were eating. I think about all the times we had sleepovers and shared secrets and played Barbies.

How did someone who used to be good turn bad so fast?

Before I can stop it, the anger erupts out of my mouth. "Shut up," I say to Karen. My voice is shaky and doesn't even sound like mine. Only problem is, Mrs. Garvin thinks I'm talking to her. She sighs loudly and rolls her eyes toward the ceiling. The look on her face says, Here we go again.

Uh-oh.

Bringing her eyes back down to me, she raises a thick finger and points it toward the door. "To the hallway, young lady."

"No, please. I wasn't — "

"Now, Miss Bennett."

Of course, Karen doesn't get in trouble for what she said. She never gets in trouble because ever since she turned popular, she's been one of Mrs. Garvin's pets. It's only ten thirty in the morning and already this day couldn't possibly get any worse. Bypassing my regular spot in the hallway, I go straight to the girls' bathroom. I lock myself in the end stall, clamp a hand over my mouth and let out a silent scream. When I'm done, I feel a bit calmer. But I'm still not ready to leave the privacy of the bathroom to go sit in that hallway. So I take a seat on the toilet and read over the collection of graffiti decorating the stall.

Rule the school.

Jenny loves Davey.

Down with disco.

Bikini Fiorini. (This one is right above a doodle of our principal wearing a frilly two-piece bathing suit.)

It's only after I finish reading all the graffiti that I realize I'm still clutching my freshly sharpened #2 pencil in my right hand. I hate writing. And I know graffiti is wrong. But something powerful is calling on me to add my own message to this bathroom stall. Leaning forward, I find a nice blank spot and add my own scrawl to the jumble of words.

I want to disapeer.

I write it really, really small. Like a whisper in a dark room.

It's just a tiny rebellion. But it helps.

After school, I don't go right home. Instead, I walk to Pinky's house and ring the doorbell. I want to ask if she ended up coming to school today. I want to ask her why she never goes outside. And what her mother prays for. But nobody answers. I ring it again. And then I put my ear to the door and listen hard. Call me crazy, but I'm sure I hear someone breathing on the other side. That, and the distinctive squeak of a thumb being sucked.

"Pinky? Padma? Are you there?" I say.

And then I hear the sound of bare feet running away across the hardwood floor.

Why won't they open the door? Is it some kind of a game? Like a reverse Nicky Nicky Nine Doors?

I reach into my schoolbag and take out a piece of notepaper, a pencil and the Fig Newtons I saved from my lunch today. From Finch, I write. Then I fold the notepaper around the cookies and slide the whole thing through the narrow mail slot on the door.

At dinner, Mom tells me she's got the TV fixed, so I better not go breaking it again or next time she'll take the handyman's bill out of my allowance. I gobble down my fish sticks, race downstairs and turn on the TV, hoping to catch up on some of my favorite shows. But instead of Laura, Mary and Nellie Oleson, there's a breaking news story flashing across the screen.

It's Terry Fox.

He's crying.

He has to stop running. His cancer has spread.

"Now I've got cancer in my lungs," he says into a bouquet of microphones.

Like Daddy, I think.

I cry along with Terry for a few seconds. And then I snap off the TV because I don't want to watch anymore. I feel so sad about this news. I can't explain why because I've never even met Terry Fox, but somehow this feels almost as bad as the day we buried Daddy. Like my heart just broke all over again.

I go upstairs to my room and shut the door. I reset my clock to 7:00 a.m., close the curtains, lie down on top of my quilt and squeeze my eyes shut. And then I wish really, really hard that when I open them it'll be this morning all over again. And that this awful day didn't actually happen.

It doesn't work.

That night, I dream about my feathers. They've grown in all white and fluffy and smooth. And I'm happy because it means I'm finally able to fly away. I spread my feathered arms and fly up, up, up to where I think I'll find heaven ... where I know I'll find Daddy. The air is cold and black all around me and I fly so high, my head gets dizzy. But I keep going. I fly until my arms are tired and feel like they'll fall off. But I keep going. I won't stop until I find Daddy.

I don't remember what happens after that in my dream. But when I wake up the next morning the muscles in my arms are aching. And my pillow is wet.

CHAPTER 6

Next day in Mrs. Garvin's class, we have to write another paragraph. This one's supposed to be about "My Sixth-Grade Goals." As soon as she announces it, I feel that awful itchy heat start to come back and I put my hand up for a bathroom break. Once I'm there, I splash some cool water over my arms and face. Then I go straight to the end stall and sit down, feeling a little bit guilty for lying because I don't really have to go. I just needed to get away from that awful classroom. I scan the wall for new graffiti, and you'll never imagine my surprise when I see a message waiting for me right under the note I wrote yesterday. The one about wanting to disappear. There it is, written in bold black marker, as clear as day — a message for me.

Don't.

I stare at the word for a full minute. It's just one word. But it sparks a little light of hope inside me. I wonder who wrote it. I wonder if it's a girl my age. Maybe even someone I know?

That afternoon, I ask Mrs. Garvin for permission to use the bathroom again. "The diarrhea in her brains must be spreading to her butt," Karen whispers to Shawna as I pass by their desks. I ignore the giggles that follow me as I make my way out of the room. This time I bring a pencil with me so I can write back. I lock myself into the end stall and wait until I'm sure I'm alone. Then I adjust my pencil grip and add my secret thoughts to the message chain.

I hate it heer.

I write the words a bit bigger this time. Then I lean back and look at what I've done. I've never liked writing. But I love the look of my confession on that bathroom stall.

When I get home from school, Mom's not in her figuring-out chair. And her car is gone from the garage. I drop my schoolbag in the front hall. My shoulder sags with relief.

Wherever Mom went, I'm just glad she didn't take me with her. I don't like riding in that old car. It makes awful clunking noises and the tires squeal every time it turns a corner. Plus, it's especially bad on hot days like today when the black vinyl seats bake in the sun and burn the backs of my legs.

Maybe she's out looking for a job, I think. A new job would be great. My heart does a Snoopy dance just thinking about it. I want my old mom back so badly. I think a new job would help.

There's nothing good on TV, so after I eat a couple of Fudgee-Os, I head to the bathroom, strip down to my underwear and look at myself in the big mirror that hangs behind the door. I step up really close, searching for signs I might be changing like Karen or Shawna did over the summer. We're the same age, after all. So how come they both look so much older than me? I search in every corner and crease, but there are absolutely no new lumps or bumps or strange little hairs that I can see. Just the same freckly, knobby-kneed, ribs-sticking-out, skin-and-bones body I've always had. I take a few minutes to search my neck and arms for new feathers, but there are none of those either. I don't know if I'm happy or sad about that. As much as I can't wait for the rest of my feathers to grow in, the idea of it makes me feel a bit nervous. What if they grow in while I'm at school? What if they grow over my face, too? What if the other kids call me a freak? Karen and her Jordache-jeans-wearing friends would have a field day with something like that.

I pull the elastics out of my brown hair and shake it loose. It falls just a smidgen shy of my shoulders … like a little kid's dangling legs, too short to reach the floor. I turn my head from side to side, as if the answer to my problems might be there if I check from a different angle. What if I tried wearing lip gloss like Karen? Would Mom get mad and make me take it off? Or would she even notice? Either way, I don't think I want to. The thought of having sticky pink lips all day isn't a nice one. I push my hair away from my face. What if I tried wearing it back in barrettes? Would that make me look better? Or older? Or would it make me look young, like Pinky? I liked the ribbon barrettes she was wearing in her hair the day we met. Maybe I could make some of those for myself. It probably can't be too hard. Laura Ingalls probably made her own hair ribbons.

Mom is home by the time I get out of the bathroom. I find her sitting at the kitchen table in front of a tall stack of unopened mail. There's a bag of groceries on the counter and a glass of ice water on the table beside her.

"Where were you?" I ask, pulling up a chair. I

put my arms around her and give her a hug. Really gentle, though. Her body's so thin, it feels like she could snap if I hug too hard.

She jingles the ice cubes around and around in her glass. "Just out."

I wait for her to say something more about it, but she doesn't. "I thought maybe you found a job," I say, hopefully. My voice is so small and squeaky, I don't even recognize it.

Mom takes a sip from her glass. She sighs. "Can we talk about something else, honey?"

"Okay. But why?"

She shakes her head while she taps her last cigarette loose from the gold-and-silver package. "Times are tough right now, Finch," she says, popping the corky-looking end in her mouth. "There *aren't* any jobs."

And then she flicks the wheel of her lighter. So casually. Like she's snapping her fingers to an old song. Like what she just said didn't make my heart drop through the floor.

No jobs? Anywhere? That can't be true. How are we going to live if Mom doesn't get a job?

I stare into those big blue eyes of hers, searching for something to tell me it's going to be all right. She stares back at me, her expression as blank as blind

Mary Ingalls's. I jump to my feet, grab the grocery bag off the counter and peer inside.

Five more boxes of frozen fish sticks. Each one marked with a blood-red sticker. *Buy Four, Get One Free.*

"Your brother said he's going to be home for dinner tonight," Mom says. "I thought I'd make his favorite."

My mouth opens, but no words come out. How can she be serious? How can she serve us fish sticks *again*? Are we that low on money? Or is there a secret ingredient in cigarettes that makes you lose your marbles?

Surprisingly, Harrison's in such a good mood tonight that he doesn't say a word about the crummy fish-stick dinner. Instead, he natters on about a new kid in his class named Albert who moved here from Montreal over the summer and who's got a Ping-Pong table in his basement and a swimming pool with a diving board in his backyard and a golden retriever named Nacho. Albert invited Harrison over to swim tomorrow after school. It hits me that this is the first time I've seen my brother so happy in months. It reminds me of the times when we used to be closer, before Daddy died, and it makes my anger melt away a bit.

Okay, a lot.

Okay, I guess I'm talking to him again.

At least one of us met a new friend, I think.

After dinner, I go to his room to talk about Mom. He's lying on top of his rumpled Star Wars sheets, listening to music on the new Sony Walkman he bought with the pile of paper route money he'd been saving for five years. I'd like a Walkman, too, but I don't have enough money to buy one, and you can bet Mom isn't going to give it to me if she's worried about the cost of fish sticks.

I wave my hands and poke the air around my ears until Harrison sees me and clicks the music off.

"What?" he says, pulling down his headphones.

"I'm worried about Mom," I reply, closing the door behind me so she won't overhear. I wait to see if Harrison says something like, "Yeah, me too" or "I know what you mean." But he just shrugs and gives me one of those Get-to-the-point-fast-before-I-kick-you-out-of-my-room looks. So I do.

"She told me there are no jobs anywhere," I say. "She just sits in that chair and smokes all day. It's like she's not even inside her own body half the time. You know what I mean?"

Harrison shakes his head. "She's fine. She's still getting over losing Dad."

I stare at him in surprise. *She's fine? How can he say that?* "Really? Then how do you explain the fish-stick situation? She told me tonight it's your favorite dinner."

He shrugs. "Give her a break, Finch. She's just got her mind on other things ..."

I wipe away the tear that's spilling down my cheek. "Well, it's been nine months already," I say. "How much longer till her mind comes back to us?"

"I don't know. I think it's different for everyone." His face softens a bit. "She'll be okay. Quit worrying. Now, scram."

He hands me a tissue for my face. But before I can say thank-you, he puts his headphones back over his ears, pushes Play and closes his eyes.

And that's that.

CHAPTER 7

There's a new message waiting for me in the end stall today. It's written in the exact same black marker as the last one, so I can only guess it's from the same person. This time, it's three words:

Me too sometimes.

And beside it, there's a frowny-face doodle.

I read it over and over again. Okay, I know this isn't exactly like having a *real* friend. But this is by far the closest I've been in months. Somebody out there in this school heard me. And she feels the same way I do. And she wants me to know about it.

This makes me happy.

So what do I do now? I'm almost afraid to take this message-writing thing any further, just in case I mess it up. But I can't help myself — I have to write something back. I can't leave the message chain hanging like this. Can I?

Just once more and then my days of graffiti will be over.

Promise.

I think for a minute. Then I pull out my pencil.

Whoo are you?

I leave the bathroom with a smile on my face. Even if the other girl doesn't write back to tell me her name, I think it's okay. And even though Mrs. Garvin gave me a D on my paragraph about "My Sixth-Grade Goals," I'm still smiling when the final bell rings. I'm happier than I've felt in weeks. I want to share my happiness with someone. On the way home, I decide to try Pinky one more time. I ring the doorbell and wait. But, just like last time, there's no answer. Where could they be? The white Chevrolet isn't in the driveway. Are they picking up Pinky from the Hindu school? Or maybe they went on a trip? Maybe they drove to Niagara Falls like my family did the weekend I was turning eight and Mom decided it was high time I saw something big and important. I put my ear to the door. But all I hear is the hush of utter silence.

To my surprise, there's a big green apple sitting on our front doormat when I get home. Someone's tied a red hair ribbon in a neat bow around the stem.

There's no note saying who it's from, but I have a guess.

Did Pinky leave this for me? As a thank-you for the Fig Newtons?

I don't know if it's true or not, but the thought makes me smile. I pick up the apple, slip the ribbon into the pocket of my jacket and go inside. Mom is taking a nap, so I go to the kitchen to eat my snack and I discover a new pile of mail on the kitchen counter. It's been dropped right beside the pile of mail Mom left there yesterday. I pour myself a cup of Kool-Aid, sit down at the table and look over the letters, checking to see if there's anything for me. None of the letters have been opened. And three of the envelopes are stamped with the words *Final Notice.*

That doesn't sound good.

Those ones are addressed to Mom, and I know it's not okay to open another person's mail, so I don't. Instead, I hold those letters up to the kitchen window, hoping I might be able to read a few words and understand what they're all about. But either the light's too dim or the paper's too thick, 'cause I can't read a thing. I drop them back in the pile and pick up another letter. This one has the words *NOTICE OF DEFAULT* in big red letters across the top. It's addressed to Bennett.

Technically that's me, I think. I'm a Bennett. Before I lose my nerve, I slide my thumbs under the flap and rip open the envelope. My eyes skim down the page.

Dear Mrs. Bennett,

This letter is a formal notification that you are in default of your mortgage (account #479279). This account has been overdue for 90 days and previous requests to reconsolidate this debt have been ignored. Unless the total amount ($1,625.34) is received within 30 days, we have no choice but to begin the foreclosure process on your home.

The letter falls to the floor along with my cup of cherry Kool-Aid. I jump up to clean the mess and all the while my brain is racing with questions.

Foreclosure? Default? Reconsolidate this debt? What exactly do those words mean? Are we going to lose our house? I wish I had a dictionary handy.

The doorbell rings just as I finish wiping the last drops of the Kool-Aid off the letter. I fold it up, stuff it into the waistband of my shorts and pull my T-shirt down over it so nobody will see what I've done. Then I go to answer the door, but I freeze when I see who's there. It's awful Matt. He's scowling down at me from the front porch.

"Harrison's not here," I say, staying well back behind the safety of the screen door.

He shakes his head as if I've just spoken in a foreign language. "What do you mean? Where is he?" he demands.

"At a friend's house."

Matt looks stunned. Like I've punched him or something. "Whose house?"

That's when it hits me. Maybe Matt doesn't have any other friends. Maybe he needs Harrison as much as Harrison needed him. "None of your beeswax," I say.

He stares at me silently for a few seconds. Then he leans forward, his shoulder falling against the door frame with a thump. "Okay, so invite me in anyway. We could hang out. You and me." His lips curl into a hideous pee-colored smile.

Matt wants to spend time with me? My stomach turns at the thought.

"No thanks!" I say quickly, reaching out to close the front door. Matt's eyes narrow. Before I know what's happening, he's pulling the screen door open and shoving me to the side. "Hey!" I squeal as he muscles past me.

"I'm coming in," he says, marching straight to our living room and flopping down on the couch. I follow along behind him, scrambling to find my voice.

"What are you doing?" I finally manage to sputter. "I told you my brother's not here."

He crosses one dirty sneaker over the other, right on top of those sky-blue cushions the old Mom used to be so careful about keeping clean. "I don't mind waiting," he says, reaching for a section of yesterday's newspaper, folded up and lying on the coffee table. "I've got time. And nothing else to do anyway."

He opens up the paper. Terry Fox's face stares out at me from the front page. *Marathon of Hope Comes to an End*, reads the headline. I close my eyes and take a deep breath.

"This isn't *your* home, Matt," I say, pushing the words out as loud and strong as I can manage. "You can't just be here uninvited."

He drops the newspaper and stares at me in surprise. "Really? Well, who's going to stop me, Flinch?"

I don't know what to say to that. I don't know what to do now. Matt's bigger and stronger and meaner than me. I don't want him in my house for another minute, but there's nobody here to help get him out. What if I called the police? Would Detective Kroon come to help? Could he arrest Matt for trespassing?

"Come on, little girl. Kick me to the curb, why don't you?" he taunts, grinning at me with those awful yellow teeth.

My palms suddenly feel wet. I glance toward the staircase, wondering if I should run and wake up Mom. Would she help me get rid of Matt? Would she even care that he's pushed his way into our home?

Matt's eyebrows arch. Ever so slowly, he swings his legs off the couch and stands up. "There's nobody here to save you, is there, Flinch?" he says quietly, taking a step toward me. I take a step back. I can hear my heart thumping in my ears. "Where's your mom?" he asks.

I move to the other side of the room, making sure to keep the coffee table between us. "She's right upstairs," I say. I don't mention anything about her being asleep.

Matt smirks. "Good. So we have time to play a fast game. This one's called Kiss the Matt."

What? But there's no time for questions because now he's lunging toward me, hands outstretched. I scream and race away toward the kitchen. If I can get to the phone, I'll be okay. At this point, calling

Detective Kroon seems like a really good plan. I stumble once but find my footing again quick enough. Still, Matt manages to catch up to me just as I reach the kitchen. I cringe when I hear his footsteps thundering behind me. I shriek when I feel the wet heat from his breath on my neck. But a second later I'm saved when the screen door opens and Harrison strides into the house clutching a wet towel. His shaggy brown hair is still damp from Albert's pool. In my whole life, I've never been so happy to see my brother. His eyes narrow when he spots me and my panicked face. And they narrow even more when he spots awful Matt stopped short behind me, panting like a hound on the chase.

"Hey, what are you doing here?" Harrison asks. His words come out slow and careful ... like he's tiptoeing around broken glass.

Matt's hands fly up, all innocent-like. "Waiting for you, man. We were supposed to hang out today."

A few seconds go by when nobody says anything. Then Harrison comes to stand beside me. "Finch?" he says quietly. "Everything all right?"

I'm just about to speak up when Mom walks into the kitchen, her face and neck creased pink from the bedsheets. Her gaze jumps from Matt to me, then to Harrison, and then back to Matt. Her eyes go wide with question marks. For the first time in months, she actually looks awake.

She takes my hand and tugs me to her side. "Did I hear a scream down here?" she asks. Her usually soft voice is edged with steel.

Matt's answer comes too loud and too quick. "Yeah. We were just playing tag. Right, Finch?"

The noise of his voice hurts my ears. Instead of an answer, I stick out my tongue at him. His eyes go dark and I move closer to the safety of Mom. I'm glad she's here. My heart is gradually slowing back down to normal, even though the NOTICE OF DEFAULT letter stuck into my waistband is digging painfully into my skin. I'm itching to ask her about it, but I don't want to do that with Matt and Harrison standing right there listening.

Mom puts her thin arm around me. She smiles at Matt, but it doesn't come anywhere close to reaching her eyes. "I was just about to start getting dinner. We're having fish sticks tonight. Would you like to join us?"

My stomach does a little flip. This is the closest she's sounded to the old Mom in ages. Except for the fish-stick thing.

"Actually, I think I better go. My folks are expecting me." He turns and pokes Harrison in the arm. "You coming?" he says under his breath.

My brother glances at me and at Mom, then his eyes turn toward the floor. To my surprise, he gives his drooping head a shake.

"Sorry. Fish sticks are my favorite. I wouldn't want to miss them."

CHAPTER 8

First thing this morning, Mrs. Garvin catches me daydreaming. She taps her ruler on my desk to "wake me up," then sends me to the office to hand in the attendance (which everyone knows is just an excuse for her to get rid of me for a few minutes). I take my time walking down the hallway, carefully stepping over all the dark lines in the tile flooring.

Step on a crack, break your mother's back. Step on a line, break your mother's spine.

Last thing I need right now is for anything bad to happen to Mom.

When I get to the office, I'm surprised to see the principal sitting behind the secretary's desk.

"Morning," she says, barely glancing up from the stack of papers in front of her.

"Hi, Mrs. Fiorini," I reply. The bikini doodle from the bathroom flashes through my head and I have to swallow my giggle. I hand her the attendance list. "Where's Mrs. Epstein?"

She takes it from me and drops it on top of a pile next to the typewriter. "Gone," she says with a huff. "Quit. Her husband's been transferred to Seattle and they're moving out there next week."

I shuffle my feet between the lines of the tiles, trying to think of something smart to say. "So, are you going to be the secretary now, too?"

"I am for the next couple of days at least. Until I can find a replacement." Her voice is grumpy. I can tell she's not happy with Mrs. Epstein.

The wheels in my head start to turn. "Well, I might know someone —"

But the phone rings before I can finish. She scowls and reaches to pick it up. "Roseborough Public School, Gina Fiorini speaking." It's not even nine thirty in the morning, but she sounds like she's ready for this day to be over. I tiptoe out of the office before she decides to aim her grump my way.

"Finch?"

I pause in the doorway and turn back around. Mrs. Fiorini's hand is covering the mouthpiece of the phone. Her dark eyebrows are pinched over the bridge of her nose.

"I've been meaning to ask ... how are you and Harrison doing these days?"

Her voice is soft and full of pity and it makes me

want to cry. I have to bite the inside of my cheek to stop myself. *It's horrible that you don't have a daddy anymore,* is what she really means. I glance down at the floor. I wish I could tell her about what's going on at home with Mom. Mrs. Fiorini's a principal, after all. Maybe she could help.

But then Mom's voice pops into my head, loud and clear as a bell. *You shouldn't be telling people my business, Finch.* And when I finally open my mouth to answer the question, I just can't bring myself to let out the truth. "We're okay, thanks," I mumble.

Mrs. Fiorini smiles and nods and goes back to her phone call. I rush out of the office before she can ask me any more questions.

You can bet I'm in no hurry to go back to class, so I decide to duck into the girls' bathroom to check for a message from my new "friend." To my shock, there's a whole crop of fresh graffiti decorating the space under where I wrote *Whoo are you?* last time I was here.

Farrah Fawcett
The Wizard of Oz
Your teacher ... spell much?
Queen Elizabeth

The girl who just ate lunch here.

This last note was written with a familiar black marker. Yeah, I'm sure this one's from my "friend." I stare at it for a few minutes, wondering what it means. Did she really eat lunch here in this stall? That's kind of terrible. Or maybe it's a joke? On my way back to class, I think about coming to check the bathroom at lunchtime in case she's there again. But in the end, I'm too afraid to do it. What if it's really just Karen or Shawna or another one of those mean Nellie Oleson–type girls playing a trick on me? I don't think I could stand it.

When lunchtime comes, I walk to the farthest corner of the school yard and eat under the shade of a tree where nobody can see me. I run my fingertip over the tiny scar on the back of my neck and pretend my lunch box is really an old-fashioned tin lunch pail. And that my Wonder Bread jam sandwich is really Ma's homemade brown bread with raspberry preserves. And that it's delicious. And that life is simple.

Mom's smoking in the kitchen when I get home from school. The pile of unopened letters on the counter looks taller than it did yesterday. I grab a Fudgee-O and sit down beside her.

"Guess what?" I say.

Mom turns to look at me. I wait a few seconds for her to say, "What?" She doesn't, but I tell her anyway.

"Mrs. Epstein, the school secretary, quit her job. Mrs. Fiorini told me they're looking for a replacement, and I'm pretty sure you don't need to take a test or do homework for answering the phone and typing, so —" I pause here to take a breath "— I think you should go and ask for the job."

Mom's eyebrows float up her forehead. She smiles a tiny smile, like she's thinking of some private joke. Her eyes flick to the window, and she takes another puff of her cigarette. I nibble on my cookie while I wait to hear what she's going to say.

"Well?"

"Thank you, honey," she finally replies, turning to blow the smoke over her shoulder. "But I don't think I'm ready to be a secretary."

I think my mouth must have fallen open, because there's a little mess of chewed-up cookie crumbs on the table under my chin where there wasn't a minute ago. Not ready? What in the world does that mean? I wait for Mom to explain, but of course she doesn't.

"I don't get it," I say. "You told me there are no

jobs ... but I found one for you this morning. Why don't you take it?"

Mom looks surprised. She gives her head a little shake. "I just told you, I'm —"

"And what about those bills?" I demand, pointing to the stack of mail she's been ignoring all week. "How are we going to pay them if you don't get a job?" My voice is rising louder and louder with every word. I feel horrible, but I can't seem to stop myself. Laura Ingalls never once raised her voice at Ma. What am I doing?

Mom runs a pale hand through her hair. The long ash end of her cigarette crumbles to dust on the tabletop, but she doesn't notice. "You don't have to worry about bills, Finch," she says. "I'll take care of them. Like I told you, I'm figuring things out."

I stand up now. My voice feels way too big for sitting down. "No, you're not!" I shout. "You're not figuring *anything* out! You're just afraid!" Tears I didn't even know I was crying stream down my cheeks and into my mouth. I'm hysterical now, but I can't stop. It's like a wild animal has taken over my body. Without thinking, I reach out and pluck the cigarette from Mom's mouth, stomp over to the sink and hurl it down into the garbage disposal.

"Finch Anne Bennett!" Mom's yelling now, too.

Good. I haven't seen her this worked up in months. Maybe not since Daddy died. But I don't care. Before she can stop me, I grab the rest of her cigarettes and throw them into the sink. I toss her lighter in, too. It clatters angrily against the stainless steel.

Now Mom's hands are gripping my shoulders, turning me around, shaking me. "Good grief! What's gotten into you?" she shouts. But I can barely hear her because I'm screaming. Like the wild animal inside me thinks if it gets loud enough, maybe it can claw deep into this new Mom and pull the old one out.

I squeeze my eyes shut because it's easier to be brave when you don't have to watch what's in front of you. "I know why you keep giving us those awful fish sticks every night 'cause I opened the default letter from the bank and I'm not sure what *foreclosure* means but I'm scared they want to take away our house and I'm even more scared because you're not doing anything about it! And Mrs. Garvin hates me and calls me stupid in front of all the other kids and I think I'll die if I have to stay in her class another day and I don't have any friends left because she turned them all against me! And I have nobody to talk to about any of this because Harrison's always hanging out with awful Matt and all you do is sit in the green chair and stare out the window!"

I pause for a second to catch my breath. But it's like all my energy has flown away with those angry words, because when I start talking again, my screams have shrunk to whispers. "And sometimes I feel like you've gone and died, too," I say, trembling 'cause these are the words that hurt the most. "And I need you to be alive."

Now the whisper is gone, too, and I'm finally quiet. All that's left is a loud ringing in my ears and a pain in my chest where it feels like I've been kicked. I open my eyes and look up at Mom. She's watching me carefully. Her eyes are bright and clear, just like they used to be before Daddy died. Nothing in there but the raw naked truth.

"I'm sorry, Finch," she says, and I can tell by her voice that she is hurting, too. It's not a lot. But it's all I need to hear before I let her cover me with a hug.

My exhausted body sags with relief in her arms.

I knew she wouldn't leave me forever.

CHAPTER 9

Halfway through the morning, Mrs. Garvin's class phone rings. She listens for a minute and when she hangs up, she walks straight to my desk and says, "Pack your things, Miss Bennett. You've just been transferred." Her voice sounds gushy, like she's relieved.

Transferred? My heart does a little cartwheel.

"Thanks," I say, pushing my stuff into my bag. I'm sure this must be Mrs. Garvin's doing. She probably hated having me in her class for two years straight and asked Mrs. Fiorini to fix it. I don't mind, of course. I'm just so excited to be free from her.

"Loser," Karen whispers as I pass her desk. But I'm so happy, even she can't ruin it. I walk down the hallway to the other sixth-grade class and knock softly on the door. My new teacher is smiling when she opens it.

"Welcome, Finch. I just got the call that you'll be joining us."

She says her name is Miss Rein. She has green eyes, freckles and red feathered hair that's the same color as a brand-new penny. I step inside the room, glancing quickly at the blur of curious faces all staring at me like I'm here to put on a show. Miss Rein steers me to an empty desk at the front of the class.

"Have a seat and make yourself at home."

At home? In school? I wonder if that's supposed to be funny. I wonder if she's waiting for me to laugh. Just in case, I smile as I sink into the chair, even though I feel nervous about sitting all the way up here. But I don't want to cause trouble for my new teacher by asking to move.

"Before we do anything else, I'd like to know a bit more about you, so maybe you wouldn't mind writing me a short biography," she says. "The rest of the students wrote theirs yesterday, but there's time this morning for you to do one, too."

"A biography?" I squirm in my seat. Why did I think those were just for famous people?

Miss Rein nods. "Yes. I'd like you to write a story about Finch Bennett's life ... just so I can get to know you better. It doesn't have to be long."

I pull my pencil case out of my bag slowly, worrying about what my new teacher will say when she sees my writing. And I worry the kids in this new class will think I'm slow. And that everyone will be watching me when I make mistakes because I'm sitting all the way up here in the front. Trying to remember all of Daddy's advice, I open to a blank page in my notebook and pick up my pencil.

> Finch Bennett is 11 yeers old. she has a mother and a brother and she had a father but he dide last yeer. Finch isint good at sports and she hates riting about herself. She likes chocolit, waching tv and lisining to music. if she culd run across the contry to help Terry Fox finish his marithon she wuld.

I take a lot of time getting the words down, but Miss Rein doesn't hurry me. I hand it in just before lunch. She reads it at her desk while I doodle on my pencil case and wait for her to start in on me about my writing. But to my surprise, she doesn't say a thing. When the lunch bell rings, she waves me down on my way out the door.

"Would you mind staying back a minute to chat, Finch?"

Oh, boy. Here it comes. I wait beside her desk, shuffling my feet while the rest of the kids push out into the hallway. She only starts talking when the last kid is out the door, which makes me pretty sure she's planning on doing some yelling.

"I read your biography. I'm very sorry to hear about your father."

"Thanks," I say quietly, staring down at the scuff marks on my shoes.

"I taught your brother, Harrison, when he was in sixth grade. How is he doing?"

"Fine, thank you," I say, wondering when she's going to get to the yelling.

She pauses and hands me back my biography. There's a note written at the top in red marker. It says, *Nice effort*. I stare up at her in shock.

"Tell me something. How do you like writing, Finch?"

"I hate it." Each word is like a knife slicing through the quiet of the classroom.

Miss Rein nods like she's not surprised to hear it. "Well, maybe we can find a few ways to make it a bit easier for you. I have some ideas. But most important, I want you to know that I'm here to teach you, not to trap you. If for whatever reason you're having trouble writing down your answers, we can always go over them at lunch or after school."

It takes me a full minute to get my voice working. "Okay," I finally say.

She opens her desk and pulls out a small bowl of Hershey's Kisses. "I like chocolate, too," she whispers, like we're sharing a secret. She holds it out for me to take one.

"Thank you," I say, smiling.

I let the chocolate kiss melt slowly in my mouth as I make my way across the school yard. My heart is racing like I've just won a lottery or something. *Nice effort.* Just two little words, but they make me feel smarter. I can't remember the last time any of my teachers made me feel smart. My insides are all puffed up and proud, and I think if I tried right now I could swim across Lake Ontario, or climb Mount Everest, or fly to the moon. I'm too excited to be hungry, but I pick at my lunch under the shade of the tree. While I eat, I watch Karen and Shawna walking arm in arm around the edges of the school yard, circling the rest of us like a pair of sharks looking for their next meal. I feel jealous watching them together. Don't get me wrong, I wouldn't want Karen for a friend anymore, even if she got down on her hands and knees and begged me. But it sure would be nice to have someone to sit with and talk to at lunch and recess. I'm halfway through my jam sandwich when I remember the message chain on the bathroom wall and the mystery girl who wrote to me. Would she be there again right now? Should I go check? After what happened this morning in Miss Rein's class, I'm feeling brave enough to try.

Before I can change my mind, I'm packing up my food and marching back into the school. The door to the end stall is closed. Someone's in there. Leaning over, I see a pair of feet wearing dusty white sneakers and blue pompom socks. I hesitate for just a second before knocking.

"Hello?" I say.

The door slowly swings open. There she is, sitting on top of the toilet seat with her lunch box in her lap as she finishes the last bites of an apple. She looks up at me; her mouth is shiny with juice.

"Pinky?" I blink a couple of times just in case my eyes are playing tricks on me. I guess I'd pretty much given up on the idea I was ever going to see her at my school. After a second, she lifts her hand and waves shyly. She's wearing a plaid dress that reminds me of the curtains in our kitchen, and her glossy hair is hanging in two perfect braids on either side of her head.

"Hi, Finch," she says with a tiny smile.

I open my mouth to speak, but nothing comes out. It's like my tongue is stuck or something. I'm really nervous I might ruin this by saying the wrong thing, which probably explains why I can't bring myself to say anything at all.

"Don't you talk?" she asks.

"Yeah," I somehow manage to answer. Where's all that courage I was feeling just a few minutes ago? "Hi," I finally say. My head is swimming with so many questions, I don't even know where to start. *Did your family take a trip? Why aren't you answering your door? Why don't you ever come outside? What happened to Hindu school?* "What are you doing here?" I ask instead. Better to start with the easy questions and work my way up.

"I go to school here," she says softly. "Miss Rein's my teacher, too. I saw you come in to class this morning — I waved, but you didn't see me."

"You go here?" I stare at her in surprise. "But I've never seen you walking to school in the morning. Or walking home either."

She wraps the apple core neatly inside a paper napkin so tight it looks like a miniature mummy in her hands. "That's because Father drives me every day. And Mother makes me run straight home as soon as the bell rings. No stopping."

I shake my head, trying to make sense of what she's saying. "But what about at lunchtime? Or recess? How come I've never seen you then?"

"I spend them here." She nods in the direction of our message chain.

"But why?"

Pinky shrugs her narrow shoulders. Her big brown eyes drop to the floor.

"I waited for you the first day of school. I wanted to walk with you." I don't mean for this to come out like I'm upset. But I think it does.

"I know. I saw you from my window," she says.

"So why didn't you come out, then?"

Pinky shrugs again.

"And I came by to see you," I say after a minute. "I came by a few times. I rang your doorbell, but nobody ever answered."

"I know," she replies. "Thank you for the cookies," she adds quietly. And that's all. I can't remember the last time I felt so confused.

"Wanna go outside and play hopscotch?" I say, changing strategies.

Her eyes are stuck to the lunch box in her lap. "I don't think I should. Father always tells me not to talk to anyone at this school. Except for the teachers, of course."

Not talk to anyone? Why? Is that the reason she spends all her time in the bathroom stall? I think about our message chain, and I get why she hates it here if she has to spend every lunch and recess time hiding. I'm about to ask her why her father would say something like that but stop myself before the words come out. I have a feeling she wouldn't answer anyway.

"Well, you're already talking to me," I point out. "So I think a few more minutes probably won't make a difference. Right?" She glances up at me. I can tell she wants to say yes, but something's holding her back. I reach out my hand. "Come on. It's really nice out."

She hesitates, peering around me as if to check to make sure we're alone. "Maybe my father was right about this school. There was an older boy who said horrible things to me at lunchtime on my first day here. And he pushed me into the boys' bathroom and held the door closed so I couldn't come out until the bell rang."

"That's awful! Who was the boy?"

"I don't know his name," she says, crossing her arms in front of her chest. "But I sure wouldn't want to see him again."

"Don't worry, I'll be with you if he comes back." I waggle my hand, inviting her to take it. "Two is always stronger than one."

And I guess that makes some kind of sense to

her, because Pinky nods and stands up. I don't know how it's possible, but she looks even smaller than she did the first time we met. She puts her hand in mine. We walk together down the hall. My head feels dizzy with happiness and I can barely walk straight. It's been so long since I've had a friend, I forgot how good it feels.

The sun is shining on the playground and the hopscotch grid is wide open. I tell Pinky the rules after she says she's never played hopscotch before (not even once!). And I let her go first because I want her to like me, and from what I can remember, that's what friends do. "I like your braids," I say shyly, as she balances on one foot to pick up her pebble. "They make you look like Laura Ingalls."

She slows her hops and turns to look at me. "You like Laura Ingalls?" She sounds suspicious.

"Yes," I reply, hoping it's not the wrong thing to say.

But as soon as the word is out of my mouth, her face breaks into a smile. "Me, too!"

So, of course I ask her which episode is her favorite. That makes Pinky look at me funny. "I was talking about the books," she says, and the way she says it makes me wonder if there's something wrong with the TV show.

"What's the difference?" I ask. It's my turn to go now. I throw my pebble and it lands on number seven.

"The books are the best," she says. "If you want, I can lend you mine. Mother bought them all for me when I was nine. She said I would learn about pioneers and North American history from reading them."

"Okay, thanks."

Just as I'm hopping toward my pebble, Karen and Shawna pass by. They're so close I can smell the stink of Love's Baby Soft perfume that surrounds them like a cloud.

"Look — hopscotch. How adorable," Karen says, although the way she makes the words sound tells me she wouldn't be caught on a hopscotch grid if her life depended on it. But I don't care if she thinks hopscotch is babyish. I don't care at all what she thinks anymore. Karen and Shawna — and awful Matt — can go jump off a bridge, for all I care.

Something snags in my brain. I stop mid-hop and twist around, arms teetering out at my sides and one foot tucked behind me.

"That older boy who was so mean to you — did he have yellow teeth?"

Pinky angles her face to the side, like she's

examining me for clues. "Yes ... how did you know?"

I hurry through the rest of my hops before I lose my balance and fall. "I think maybe I know who he is," I say, once I'm back to the beginning of the grid. But I don't say Matt's name out loud because I don't want to stain my new friendship with any of the bad stuff. The bell rings. "We better get to class," I say, letting my pebble drop to the concrete. Pinky looks surprised when I link my arm through hers. But then she smiles and we walk into the school together, matching our steps in perfect time like a pair of synchronized swimmers.

CHAPTER 10

All my happiness turns to worry on the way home from school. After our big talk yesterday, Mom promised she'd try to do better by me and Harrison. But what happens if I get home and find her back in the figuring-out chair and staring out the window like yesterday never happened?

I tiptoe through the door, drop my schoolbag on the floor and go looking for Mom. I find her in the kitchen. She's washing dishes over the sink, really slow like she's giving the plates a bubble bath. Her eyes are closed and her face is tilted toward the afternoon sun like a new spring flower, and she's humming that old song her and Daddy used to put on the record player and dance to in the living room on Saturday nights after they'd put me and Harrison to bed and thought we were sleeping. The stack of unopened mail on the counter has disappeared. The ashtray has been emptied. Her hair is clean and brushed and she's wearing her best pantsuit and her favorite blue eye shadow.

I freeze. Something's up.

"Mom?"

Her eyes fly open. She stops humming when she sees me standing there. "Hi," she says, pulling her hands out of the sink. She wipes them off on the daisy-printed dishtowel and walks over to where I'm standing. I peer closely at her face. Her eyes look clear as rain. I breathe a small sigh of relief.

"Guess what?" I say, wrapping my arms around her waist and burying my cheek into the softness of her arm.

She only hesitates for a second. I feel her cool, damp fingers smoothing a strand of hair away from my face. "What?"

"I got a new teacher today. Her name is Miss Rein. Harrison had her when he was in sixth grade and she's really nice."

"I already know all about it," Mom says. I look up at her face. She's smiling the kind of quiet smile that says, I know something you don't know.

"What do you mean?"

Mom and I sit down at the table and she tells me how she went to talk to Mrs. Fiorini about the problems I was having with Mrs. Garvin.

I'm gobsmacked. "You were at my school this morning?"

"I was. And your principal looked like she had her hands full in that office, so believe me, she didn't put up much of a fight when I asked if you could be transferred to the other sixth-grade class."

This must explain why she's dressed so nicely. "Did you ..." My fingers are twisting pretzel knots in my lap. I'm too nervous to finish the question.

Mom lets out a shuddery breath. "She said the job was mine if I wanted it."

I think my heart might have just stopped. "And ... do you want it?"

Mom reaches for her new lighter and the gold-and-silver package sitting on the counter. She nods. "I start next week."

Her hands are quivering a bit as she lights her cigarette. I can tell she's still scared. But I feel so proud of her for doing this.

"Now, a job will mean there's going to be a lot of changes around here," she says, blowing a puff of smoke over her shoulder. "Depending on the workload, I might not be around every day after school when you get home. Are you okay with that?"

Well, it's not like she's *really* been around much these past few months anyway. Not like she used to be. So of course I'm okay with that. I'd be okay with anything as long as it means the bank will stop sending us scary letters and we don't have to eat fish sticks anymore and my old mom is here to stay for good.

"I think we should celebrate tonight," I say.

Mom smiles. "I was just thinking the same thing." She stubs out her cigarette in the newly cleaned ashtray. "How about we do something different for dinner? Pancakes, maybe?"

It's a long way off from the big fancy meals she used to make before Daddy died. And maybe those fancy meals are gone forever. But you can bet I'm not complaining about it. I'll take pancakes over fish sticks any day.

"Sounds yummy," I say.

Mom reaches into her purse and presses a five-dollar bill into my palm. "Run to the corner store and buy me a couple of things, would you, Finch?"

It's not for cigarettes this time. Today it's for pancake essentials — a stick of butter and a carton of milk. And if there's any change left over, Mom says I can get myself a treat. I skip the whole way there, taking care not to step on a single crack or line. I freeze when I see who's standing in the middle of the candy aisle.

"Pinky?"

I can't believe this. Twice in one day? I walk over to where she's standing.

"What are you doing here?"

Turning to look at me, she waves and holds up a bottle of aspirin. "Mother's not feeling well. She sent me to buy some medicine."

"I'm here for my mom, too. We're having pancakes for dinner. Want to come join us?"

But just like with so many of my questions, Pinky doesn't reply. I wish I was smart enough to understand why. The ringing sound of the cash register fills the silence between us. I think for a minute.

"If you don't like pancakes, that's okay. Mom will probably make you something else if I ask. Or we could just play, if you want. Do you like jacks? Or maybe we could throw a Frisbee in my backyard?"

I wonder if Pinky has to go to the bathroom because she suddenly looks very uncomfortable. Her lips are twisting and squishing so much, I can't tell if she's smiling or frowning. I hope I haven't made her upset. "I can't," she finally says.

"But why?" I ask, even though I'm pretty sure she won't give me an answer. So imagine my surprise when she does.

"I'm ... I'm not allowed to go to your house," she whispers. Her eyes drop to the bottle in her hands. "Father worries about us. He doesn't want us spending time with kids he doesn't know. He thinks we're safer at home," she says, her eyes still glued to the aspirin. "He wouldn't even like it if he knew I was here with you in this store."

"Safer at home?" I can't hide my shock. What's so dangerous about coming over to my house? I scratch my head, trying to understand how this works. "But ... but how can you go to school, then?"

Her eyes jump around the store, like she's worried somebody might be listening. "My parents don't agree about school." She's speaking in a hushed voice, so I have to lean in to hear it. "Especially since I told them about that boy who was calling me names. Father got upset and said he doesn't want me going there anymore. He says no school at all would be better than one where his daughter is mistreated and made to feel ashamed. And he talks about tradition a lot. I know he wants to send me to a Hindu school, but Mother wants me to stay where I am. She wants me and Padma to be like other kids. They talk in the evenings when Father gets home from work. He says he doesn't like how people treat us in this country and thinks we should go home to India. But Mother wants to stay. She says there are many good people here, too, and that this is a better place for girls to grow up. They argue about this a lot, but I'm not supposed to hear it. They argue in their room every night." She pauses here and takes a deep breath, lifting her chin so her eyes meet mine. "My father just wants us to be happy."

These are by far the most words I've ever heard her say. Too bad I'm so confused by this conversation, I don't even know how to reply. My whole life, I've never heard of a kid not going to school. Don't all kids go to school? Don't all parents want them to? I stare closely at Pinky, trying to wrap my brain around what she's telling me. It's at that moment when I see myself right there in her face. I see a girl who's trapped in a mess of grown-up problems. A girl who's struggling just to figure it all out.

"What do *you* want?" I whisper.

"I don't want to leave." Her answer is strong and sure. She looks up at me with big eyes that could easily swallow up both of us. "I want to stay with you in Miss Rein's class. It's just hard sometimes ... being different."

Well, *that*, at least, is something I can understand.

"I think that you should tell your parents how you feel, then," I say. I point to the cash register. "Come on. Let's pay."

CHAPTER 11

Pinky and I walk up to the cash register with our stuff. After handing over Mom's five-dollar bill, I squeak with happiness when I get a handful of change back from the cashier. "This means we can get a treat," I say, jingling the coins with joy while Pinky pays for her mother's aspirin. Before she can say boo, I'm grabbing her hand and pulling her back to the candy aisle. She stands frozen beside me, her brown eyes drinking up the kaleidoscope of sweets in front of us.

"Go on," I say, nudging her forward. "Choose what you like. I have enough for both of us."

"I ... I don't know if I'm allowed ..." she starts to say. But her words dissolve like sugar in warm milk when she spots the display of rainbow-colored lollipops on the top shelf — Astro Pops, Tootsie Pops, Bubblegum Pops, Whirly Pops, Unicorn Pops. She swallows so hard, I can hear the gulp at the back of her throat.

I don't understand why she looks so nervous.

"Come on. My mom said it was okay."

I wait for her to choose something, but it's like she's superglued to that one spot. "But my parents ... I'm not sure they'll approve," she whispers.

I reach for a package of Fun Dip for myself. The cherry-and-lime combo — my all-time favorite. "It's only candy, Pinky. No big deal." When I turn back to show her, I'm surprised to see she still hasn't moved. I poke her with my elbow to get her going. "Come on. How will they know anyway?" I ask.

She doesn't answer. Her eyes just get wider.

I think for a minute. "Hey, maybe you could tell them it's a tradition to give your new neighbors some food. Mom was going to bring something over, but she never got around to it. So this would make up for that."

She glances at me. "A tradition? Really?"

I nod. "Yup. Cross my heart."

And I guess that's all Pinky needs to hear, because the words are barely out of my mouth before she's stepping forward and reaching for the lollipop closest to her, a multicolored one that has got to be the biggest on the shelf. I giggle as I watch her peel off the wrapping and take a lick. The candy is practically as big as her head.

I pay for the treats and we walk home eating them. I show her how to play the sidewalk game. "It's easy. *Step on a crack, break your mother's back. Step on a line, break your mother's spine.*" But the look on Pinky's face is filled with so much horror, for a moment I think she's going to drop her lollipop. "Well, it's not real, silly," I explain, laughing. "It's just for fun."

We spend the rest of the walk licking candy, hopping over lines and sidestepping cracks. We're almost home and I don't want our time together to end, but I can't ask her if she wants to come over to my house and play 'cause I already know what her answer would be. So I slow my steps, finish my last lick of candy and stick out my tongue. "Red or green?"

"Purple," she replies. "What color is mine?" she asks, sticking hers out, too.

I stop walking and look. "Brown," I say. "And your lips are pink and yellow." The colors remind me a bit of the elephant painting I saw in their kitchen and I tell her so. Her tongue disappears back into her mouth and her face turns serious.

"That elephant's Ganesh. He's the god of wisdom and salvation. He's very important in our religion. Mother prays to him a lot."

"Okay," I say. I'm itching to ask how an elephant can be a god but stop myself before the words come out. I can practically hear Mom's voice in my head telling me to mind my own business. "How did you do that thing with your tongue?" I ask instead. "You know, the other day in the window?"

Pinky's chin rises with pride. "Easy. Like this," she says, doing her trick again for me. I stick my purple tongue out and try to make it reach my nose, but it comes nowhere close. I try to think up something special I can show her about me.

"I had a feather once, you know. It grew out of my neck." I push my hair out of the way to show her the scar. She looks nicely impressed.

"Goodness. What does it mean?" she asks, rising onto her tiptoes to get a closer look.

"It means I'm going to fly one day," I whisper. This is a secret I've never told anyone before. But I trust Pinky not to laugh or tease. Also I figure anyone whose mother prays to an elephant will have an open mind about something like this.

We start walking again. Her father's white Chevrolet is pulling up in the driveway just as we arrive. As soon as she sees him, Pinky stops walking, hides what's left of her lollipop behind her back and grabs for my hand. She clutches my fingers hard, but I don't pull away because I get the feeling she just really needs to hold on to something. I wonder how it's possible that someone so little can be so strong. Mr. Nanda spots Pinky as he's swinging the car door shut. He starts to smile, but then his eyes fall on me and a shadow rolls over his face, like a cloud blowing across the sun. "I have to go now," Pinky says, dropping my hand. She runs past her father, straight inside her house. She doesn't look back once and she doesn't say goodbye either. Mr. Nanda follows close behind, pulling the door closed with a soft snap. Her half-eaten lollipop is lying on the sidewalk beside me, broken clean in two.

The next morning Pinky isn't in Miss Rein's class. I check the bathroom stall at recess, but she's not there either. At lunch, I check every corner of the school yard, just in case she's hiding somewhere. But she's not. She's not anywhere. It's like she's disappeared.

I find her later that day when I get home from school. She's sitting on the steps of my front porch when I walk up, and she's hugging her knees to her chest. Her face looks pale and her pretty brown eyes are rimmed with red. I drop my schoolbag on the driveway and hurry over. "Hi," I say, sitting down beside her. "I missed you at school. Are you sick or something?"

She shakes her head but doesn't offer any details. Before I can ask where she was today, she cuts in with her own question.

"I want to know — why are you so nice to me, Finch?"

I stare at her in surprise. "Because I like you, of course."

"Even though my family's Punjabi?" she asks.

"Why should that matter?"

Pinky shrugs. "Because it matters to others. A lot. That boy with the yellow teeth called me a terrible word — as if where I come from is a bad thing. And somebody spray-painted *Go home* on the front door of our old house. My parents didn't say so, but I think that's why we moved away and came here. And Father says that some people at his office speak badly of him — not to his face but loud enough so he can hear. He says they don't want him working there." She pauses for a second and takes a deep breath. "Father says it's because there are many people in this part of the world who don't like people from our part."

I bite my lip, wondering what to say to that. I feel like maybe I should apologize to her, even though I'm pretty sure I haven't done anything wrong. I don't even know anything about India.

"So why *do* you like me?" she presses.

"Well, because you're nice," I say simply. "And funny. And ... and because you like me back."

I know it's not much of an answer, but I guess maybe it's enough, because she nods and smiles and pushes a book into my hands before I can say anything more. "I have to go now, but this is for you," she says. "I was going to leave it in your mailbox, but this is better."

"Oh," I say, examining the cover. There's a picture of a brown-haired girl smiling and hugging a doll. The title says *Little House in the Big Woods*.

"It's the first Laura Ingalls book," she explains. "It's my favorite."

"Thanks." I scan the picture for anything familiar, but from what I can see, there's no prairie. There are no hair braids. No Nellie Oleson either. I glance sideways at Pinky. "Are you sure this is the same Laura Ingalls?"

"Of course I'm sure. Read it. You'll see."

"Okay," I say, putting the book on my lap. "So why weren't you at school today?"

Pinky takes a deep breath. She looks at my shoes, at her fingernails, at the brick wall behind me ... anywhere but my eyes. "I can't go back there anymore," she says in a small voice.

I stare at her in shock. "What do you mean, you can't go back? Like, ever?"

She shakes her head slowly. "Father saw me with you yesterday and he saw the lollipop colors on my mouth and he got upset that I broke the rules. He says I'm to stay at home until he figures out what to do next. He and Mother argued about it for a long time."

It suddenly feels like a giant knot is tightening inside me. *Pinky's not coming back to school?*

"But that's wrong," I say. "Every kid has to go to school. It's the law." I actually know this for a fact because of all those times last year I begged Mom not to make me go. "Can't you tell your father that?"

"No, I can't," she says. "He believes it's *his* job to protect us."

The knot pulls tighter, squeezing my stomach painfully. I'm desperate to figure out a way to make this right. "I still don't get it. Protect you from what?"

She opens her mouth to answer, but the nearby sound of a slamming car door seems to startle her.

"I shouldn't be here. I have to go," she says, ignoring my question.

"No, wait—"

Next thing I know, she's jumping to her feet. "You're nice, too, Finch," she says with a shy smile. "Bye-bye." And she's gone before I can ask anything more. I'm left sitting there on the porch, holding the Laura Ingalls book in my lap and trying to make sense out of everything that just happened.

And wondering if I'll ever see Pinky Nanda again, even though she lives right next door.

CHAPTER 12

Today is Mom's first day at her job. I know she's nervous about it because she goes upstairs to change her blouse three times in ten minutes. And she doesn't say anything at breakfast when Harrison pours practically the whole sugar bowl over his cereal. And she's clutching on to her coffee mug so hard, her knuckles turn white.

Harrison leaves for school early to meet up with Matt, so Mom and I walk together, which makes me happy because the last time she walked me to school, I think I was probably in kindergarten. She gives me a quick kiss goodbye before heading into the office.

"Wish me luck," she says. The expression on her face reminds me of the way she looked that time two summers ago when Harrison convinced her to ride a giant looping roller coaster at the carnival — like she's getting ready to puke.

"You'll be great, Mom," I say, hoping I sound

convincing enough to help. I know how scary first days can be. Daddy used to have a smart saying about staying brave, even when you're scared: *Sometimes all you can do is face the bad stuff head-on and cut a path straight through the middle.*

Pinky's not here for recess, so I play hopscotch by myself and think about how I can get her to come back to school. I'm so lost in my thoughts, I don't even notice Matt standing there. I hear his taunting voice before I actually see him.

"Hey, Flinch!"

I freeze mid-hop on the number-six square and look up. He's standing at the top of the hopscotch grid, sneering at me with his dirty yellow teeth. My heart feels like it's just flown into my throat.

"Saw you and your little friend coming out of the store last week." He yells this really loud even though I'm only a couple of feet away from him. Out of the corner of my eye, I see faces turn our way, curious to see what the commotion is about.

"Go away, Matt," I say, bringing my raised foot down with a stomp. My game of hopscotch is officially over.

"Who's going to make me?"

It doesn't take long for all the kids around us to stop what they're doing and gather to watch. The hopscotch grid has suddenly become a stage. And Matt and I are the stars of the show.

"I saw you holding hands. Are you two in love?" he asks with a laugh.

"Stop it!" I'm yelling now, too. And there's a hot, angry rash spreading up my chest.

He walks toward me, crossing over the number-ten square. Then the eight and nine squares. I glance around the crowd, hoping to find a teacher who can help before this gets any worse. I spot Harrison hanging back by the basketball net. I try to catch his attention, but his eyes are glued to the ground.

"You gonna start wearing one of those stupid dots on your forehead now?" Matt says, still walking forward. He stops when he gets to the number-seven square. He's right in front of me now, his hands clenched into fists like he's ready for a fight. I know he's waiting for me to run. Just like the time he chased me when Harrison was out swimming. And the time with the dead mouse when I jumped out the window. I take a deep breath. Maybe it's because I'm so angry, but for some reason I feel braver than I probably ought to. This time, I'm not going to let Matt see how scared I am.

"You shut up!" I shout, hoping he doesn't notice the quaver in my voice.

A look of surprise passes over his face. "What did you say, Flinch?"

The playground is deadly quiet. This is my last chance to run. I know this for a fact. But I also know that if I run away again, Matt's just going to keep on chasing me forever. *No way around this one, Finch,* Daddy's voice tells me. *Head-on and straight through the middle.*

I take two steps forward and rise up on my tiptoes so I'm looking him almost straight in the eye. "I said shut up! Go pick on someone your own size!"

The words are barely out of my mouth before Matt's hands fly out and push me hard. I go tumbling backward and fall flat on the ground, the back of my head grazing the concrete. My heart is drumming in my chest and I feel a bit dizzy, but I manage to get back on my feet. My blue cotton jacket is torn at the elbows, and under the holes I can see blood where my skin has scraped off. It takes a few seconds for my head to clear before I'm able to realize what's happening in front of me.

My brother's face is right up in Matt's and he's yelling so hard, his cheeks have gone red. "Lay off! She's half your size!"

Matt gives Harrison a hard shove. But unlike me, Harrison stays steady on his feet.

"You've changed, Harr," Matt sneers. A second later, Harrison pulls his shoulder back and throws his fist into Matt's face. Matt staggers back a couple of steps, then runs full force at Harrison and knocks him to the ground. I see bright red drops spatter on the concrete. One of them is bleeding, or maybe it's both of them, but everything's happening so fast, I can't tell. I hear someone screaming nearby and find out later that the someone was me. The kids in the school yard have formed a wide circle around them. "Fight! Fight! Fight!" they yell with perfect timing, almost as if they rehearsed this in advance. I close my eyes because it's all too awful to watch. I run my fingertips over my scar and silently pray for the rest of my feathers to grow in fast. Right here. Right now. I don't even care who sees. *I'm ready. I'm ready to fly away*, I think. In the middle of all the confusion, somebody must have gone to get help, because the next thing I know, Miss Rein is grabbing both boys by their collars and steering them into the school. I run along behind, worried about Harrison. I'm happy when I see it's Matt who's got the bloody nose.

"It's not my fault!" Matt hollers, wiping the blood away with the back of his hand. He points at Harrison. "He hit me first!"

"Only because you pushed my little sister!" Harrison yells back.

"We'll have to let the principal straighten all this out," Miss Rein says. Her eyes flicker over to me and my torn-up elbows. "It's probably a good idea if you come along, too, Finch," she says softly. "I think Mrs. Fiorini will want to hear your side of the story."

What with Matt's bloody nose, Harrison's red face and my scraped elbows, I figure we must make a pretty sorry sight as we pile into the office. Mom's sitting behind the desk, rolling a fresh sheet of paper into the typewriter when she sees us. Her face goes sickly white ... as pale as the piece of paper she's holding in her hands. "Hi, Mom," I say sheepishly. I'm guessing this isn't doing much to help her first day on the job go smoothly.

"Playground battle," Miss Rein explains, although I'm pretty sure Mom already had that part figured out. "Once I get these injuries taken care of, will Mrs. Fiorini be available to speak to these students?"

Mom nods and waves us through. She's totally and utterly speechless. I don't know if I should be relieved by her silence or scared out of my wits.

We huddle into the principal's small office. Matt (with an ice pack on his nose) stands on one side of Harrison and me on the other. Mrs. Fiorini drops her pen when she sees us. "For heaven's sake! What happened here?"

"There's been a fight. However, I'm needed back on the playground, so I'll have to leave the students to explain themselves to you," Miss Rein says, excusing herself from the room. As soon as she's gone, I don't waste any time jumping in with my side of the story.

"Matt was making fun of me and my friend and saying bad things about her and then he pushed me onto the ground and tore my jacket." I pause here to point out my scraped elbows as evidence. "Please don't be mad at Harrison ... He was just defending me. Matt pushed him, too." I've never been a tattletale before in my life. But it feels so good to tell on awful Matt.

Mrs. Fiorini turns to look at him. "Is this true?"

Of course Matt pretends to be innocent. As if he'd ever confess.

"You're going to believe her?" he scoffs, pointing a finger at me. "When I'm the one standing here with the ice pack on my nose?"

"Don't lie, Matt," I cut in. "You said mean things about Pinky. And everyone in the school yard heard you!"

Mrs. Fiorini sighs so loud, the papers on her desk

flutter from the breeze. "All right, so where is this friend right now? I'd like to hear from her as well."

I freeze like someone's just thrown a bucket of ice water at me. I wasn't expecting that. Is Mrs. Fiorini going to phone Mrs. Nanda? Because the last thing I want is for Pinky to get called into the principal's office. Imagine how upset her parents would be if that happened!

"No, you can't talk to her," I say, scrambling for a way to keep Pinky out of this. "She ... she doesn't even go to school anymore."

Mrs. Fiorini's eyes narrow. "What do you mean? How old is this girl?"

"She's eleven. Like me."

"And how do you know she doesn't go to school?"

I suddenly have a bad feeling I've said something I shouldn't have. The room goes uncomfortably quiet while everyone waits for my answer. "Because she told me so," I reply. My voice is so small, you'd think it was coming out of an ant instead of a girl.

Mrs. Fiorini takes out a fresh piece of paper and picks up her dropped pen. "All right, what's her name?" she asks.

My armpits break out in a nervous sweat. Is Pinky in trouble? What should I do now? What should I say? I don't want to make this any worse than it is.

"Finch? Can you at least tell me where she lives so I can contact her family?"

I look around for Mom, hoping she might be able to help. But the door to the office is closed.

"Answer me, Finch," says Mrs. Fiorini.

I glance over at Harrison. He's shaking his head at me like a warning. What does that mean? Answer the question? Don't answer the question? Now he's mouthing a silent message at me. What does he think I am — a lip reader? Because I don't know what else to do, I shove my hands into my jacket pockets — as if the answer might miraculously be hiding in there. It's not, of course. But my fingers close over the little ribbon Pinky tied to that perfect green apple she left on my front porch last week. And all I can think is that this must be a sign everything's going to turn out okay. I turn back to Mrs. Fiorini and open my mouth, certain the right words will somehow magically find their way out of me.

But the next words I hear end up coming from Matt.

"She lives right next door to them," he tells the principal. He looks at me and smiles his hideous smile. Then he leans in close and hisses in my ear, "Right, Flinch?"

CHAPTER 13

So Matt and Harrison are both suspended from school for three days. It doesn't matter that Harrison was defending me. Mrs. Fiorini says fighting in the school yard is absolutely against the rules, so she has no choice but to give both of them the same punishment. She looks a bit guilty about having to suspend my brother, though, and I get the feeling she only does it because the principal rule book is telling her to.

After Mrs. Fiorini calls his house, Matt's mother comes to pick him up and (from what Mom told me later) she was none too happy about it because she grabbed him by the ear and dragged him out that office door before he had a chance to try to con her with that fake innocent act of his.

Good.

Harrison had to sit in the office until Mom could take him home at the end of the school day. He tells me later that she sneaked over to give him a hug and say she's proud of him for sticking up for his sister. I hope that made Harrison feel a bit better about the whole suspension thing. It makes me feel better, at least. I tell myself to thank him later. And to ask if this fight means him and Matt aren't going to be friends anymore. My fingers are crossed on that one.

Mom walks us home at the end of the day. I have so many questions I want to ask her. I want to know what she thought of her job and if she had any trouble figuring out the electric typewriter and which kids needed late slips and which kids got detentions. I want to know if I made a mistake telling Mrs. Fiorini about Pinky and why she wanted to know her address and if she's going to get in trouble. But I zip my lips and don't ask any of it. I'm thinking she's too rattled for questions right now. Even though the whole thing was Matt's fault, I have to admit that we pretty much wrecked her first day on the job. None of us say a word the entire way home. When we get there, Harrison trudges off to his room and slams the door. Mom sinks into her figuring-out chair and lights a cigarette. I hover in front of the living-room window, watching her eyes closely and hoping they don't turn into empty swimming pools again. But she waves her hand at me and says,

"Go on, Finch. I'm fine," like she knows exactly what I'm worried about. And she does look sort of fine, all things considered. So I grab a Fudgee-O and the book Pinky gave me and head outside.

I settle into the shady spot at the side of the house and open the book. Unlike writing, reading is something I actually like. And it turns out Pinky was right — the book *is* about the same Laura Ingalls. Only she's a lot younger than she is in the TV show. So young, she hasn't even moved to the prairie yet. But Ma and Pa and Mary and Carrie are all there and even Jack the dog. I read for a long time and even forget to go inside for TV. In fact, I get so caught up in this other side of Laura's life, nothing else matters. The only thing that pulls my nose out of the book is when I hear the loud thunk of a car door slamming and notice the bright white police cruiser that's pulled up on the street in front of my house. A big, burly policeman with heavy black boots and a gun on his hip gets out and walks slowly around the back of his car, and for one awful minute I'm positive he's come to arrest me and Harrison for causing a disturbance at school today. But he doesn't come to our house, after all.

Instead, he walks across the lawn to the Nandas' front door.

And it feels like all the blood in my body is suddenly rushing to my face.

Oh, boy, this is really, really, really bad. Has he come to arrest Pinky? I shut the book with a slap and run over to the front lawn so I can see what's going on. Crouching down, I hide behind one of the prickly evergreen bushes that separate our two properties and peek through the branches at Pinky's front door. The policeman is knocking on it for what seems like a long time. Finally it opens and Mrs. Nanda steps out. She closes the door behind her, and I see that she's speaking to the policeman. Are those handcuffs hanging from his pocket? I wish I could hear what they're saying, but my heart is hammering so loud in my ears, I can't hear anything else. I hope he's not going to put Pinky in jail. I cross my fingers and wish really hard that it's going to be okay. I wanted Pinky to come back to school with me. But you can bet I never wanted her or her family to get in trouble.

They stand there on the step for a long time. Mrs. Nanda's hands are clasped together like she's praying. It looks like the policeman is doing most of the talking and she's doing most of the nodding. Every now and then, he writes something down on his notepad. Pinky's nowhere in sight. I wait in those bushes, terrified about what's going to happen next. You can't imagine how relieved I am when the policeman finally tips his cap and turns to leave. I don't dare come out of the bushes until his car is gone from our street. All I want to do is go over and find out if Pinky's okay, and before I know it I'm standing on their front porch ringing the bell. I knock, too, just in case the bell doesn't work. Nobody answers, even though I know for a fact that they're home.

"Pinky?" I say, rising up on my tiptoes and peeking into the peephole. I think I see a little flicker of light pass through the glass, but still nobody opens the door. "Are you there?" I ask, bending over, pushing open the mail slot and peering inside. A pair of familiar blue pompom socks are standing frozen on the hardwood floor.

"Go home, Finch," Pinky says through the narrow opening. "Please."

And now there's a second, larger pair of feet standing beside her and a hushed voice speaking a tangle of words I can't understand.

"Pinky?" I try again. "Can you open the door? I want to talk to you."

"No. I can't," she whispers.

"But I need to know ... what did the policeman say?"

Mrs. Nanda's voice floats through the door again. Whatever she's saying to Pinky seems to be growing more urgent.

"Mother says she will take care of it. She says thank you for coming. But to please go now."

I don't want my friend to get in any more trouble with her parents, so reluctantly I let the mail slot flap shut and head home. As soon as I'm inside, I find my schoolbag and grab a pencil and a piece of paper out of my notebook and do something I probably wouldn't have done a couple of weeks ago.

I write a letter. Yeah, without anybody forcing me to.

Deer Pinky
are you all rite? I am home if you want to tak.
call me. 555-3729
Sinceerly,
Finch

I fold the paper over, walk back to her porch and slide it through the mail slot on the door. Hopefully she'll get it. Then at least Pinky will know she's not alone. I know for a fact that will help.

When I go back inside, I find Mom leaning over the kitchen sink, grabbing on to the countertop with both hands as if she needs something to keep her from falling over. Her shoulders sag like there's something heavy sitting on them.

"Mom?"

She spins around. As soon as she sees me, she straightens her shoulders and smiles a tiny smile. "I'm thirsty," she says, grabbing a couple of empty glasses out of the drying rack. "Let's make Kool-Aid."

The afternoon and evening pass slowly. I wait close to the phone for Pinky's call. But it never comes.

When I walk into Miss Rein's class the next day, Pinky's sitting there in the front row wearing a pretty blue dress with matching barrettes in her hair. She looks a little uncertain, but her eyes brighten when she sees me, and she waves. I'm so shocked to find her sitting there, I feel like running over and giving her a big hug. But the bell has already rung and I don't want to get in trouble two days in a row, so I just wave back and take my seat. I'm so happy she's here and so relieved it all turned out okay that I don't think I even hear a single word of the lesson that morning. As soon as the recess bell rings, I jump out of my chair and run over to give Pinky that hug.

"What happened yesterday? What did the policeman say? Did you get my letter?" I ask.

She speaks really softly so that nobody but me will hear. She tells me how her parents talked in their bedroom for a long time, but the door was closed, so she couldn't make out what they were saying. "I was worried because both their voices sounded upset. But they weren't yelling, which is good," she says. "Then Father came out and spoke to me and he was very calm. Not at all angry like I thought he'd be. I've never seen him so calm. He said how he knew this day was coming. He spoke about Punjab a lot and talked about his parents' home in the country and how happy he was when he was my age. He said he's making plans and will take us on a trip there very soon but not to tell Mother because it will be a surprise. Then he tucked me into bed and told me everything was going to be all right and that I could go to school today."

I link my arm through hers and we go outside to the playground together. We play hopscotch and freeze tag, and it's the best day of school I can remember.

After the final bell I pack up my schoolbag fast,

hoping Pinky and I can maybe walk home together today. And since her father has changed his mind about school, maybe he'll change his mind about letting her come over to my house to play. But she's already gone by the time I look up, and I can't find her anywhere. I go to the office to see Mom. She says she needs a few minutes to finish up filing some papers and then we can go home together. That's when I see Mr. Nanda's white Chevrolet out the office window in the school parking lot.

"Be right back," I say, running outside so I can say goodbye to Pinky. But I get there just as the car is pulling away. I catch a quick glimpse of her in the backseat. She's watching me and waving and smiling. I wave back. One of her blue barrettes is loose and hanging down around her ear.

I go back to the office and plop down on the bench where the naughty kids sit when they're sent to see the principal.

While I wait for Mom to finish, I swing my legs back and forth, back and forth, trying to shake off the bad feeling that's suddenly creeping through my bones.

CHAPTER 14

Mom takes forever to finish up her work. When we finally get home from school, Harrison's playing basketball on the driveway. He looks relieved to see us. I wonder if he was lonely sitting at home with nothing to do for seven hours. When Mom asks him how his day went, he stops dribbling, shrugs and points his thumb back toward the house.

"Fine, I guess. But just so you know, our next-door neighbor's in the kitchen."

Mom looks at him funny. "What?"

"That little girl Pinky —" Harrison flicks his chin at me "— you know, the one Matt was making fun of? Her mom is in the kitchen."

"Why?"

"I don't know," he says, sounding annoyed. "I was watching TV and she was knocking really loud, so I came upstairs to let her in. She said she wanted to talk to Finch. I told her Finch wasn't home yet. She said she'd wait, so I made her a cup of Nescafé. She looked pretty upset."

I wonder if this is about school? Or maybe she's mad at me for telling Mrs. Fiorini about Pinky? I turn to look at Mom, wondering if she knows something I don't know. But she's obviously just as confused as me.

"Did she say anything else?" Mom asks.

"Nope," Harrison says, passing his basketball from one hand to the other.

"Let's go," Mom says, steering us inside. And just like Harrison said, there's Mrs. Nanda sitting at our kitchen table. Her head is bowed into her hands and there's a cup of instant coffee growing cold in front of her. She looks up when we come in. Her long, dark braid looks straggly today and her eyes are puffy.

"Please," she says, rising to her feet. "My daughter says you are a nice girl. A friend." Her accent is stronger than Pinky's. Her voice curls around each word.

Mom's right beside me. She puts a hand on my shoulder. "How can we help you, Mrs. Nanda?"

She walks toward me and takes my hand. Her skin is soft and smooth as sea glass. "Did you see my Pinky at school today?" she asks, her eyes searching mine.

I nod eagerly 'cause here's something I do know the answer to. "She was in my class. We played together at recess. And we ate lunch together, too."

She's hanging on to my words like they're the only things keeping her up. "She did not come home after school this afternoon. I hoped perhaps she walked with you?"

I stop nodding. "No."

Mrs. Nanda closes her eyes. A second later, she droops into the kitchen chair — like a marionette with broken strings. I wonder what's wrong. I wonder if what I said upset her. After a minute, she starts talking again.

"Last night my husband told me he wants a divorce," she says, her voice hushed like she's telling us a secret. "Because I told him I want Pinky and Padma to go to public school like other children in the neighborhood. And how I do not like how he shelters them so. This upset him."

A mess of questions is spilling through my brain, but I keep quiet, afraid to interrupt.

"This morning he was more calm and I was hoping he had changed his mind. And then this afternoon, he came early from work," she continues. "He said he was sorry for our argument and offered to take Padma to the park while I rested. But he has not brought her back. And then when Pinky did not return from school, I became very worried. I called my husband's work to ask if he had returned to the office, but ... but they told me he had quit his job." Her voice melts away. Tears are running down her cheeks now. Mom takes a seat at the table, too. She reaches into her pocket for a tissue and passes it to Mrs. Nanda. I'm still standing in the middle of the kitchen floor, frozen like a marble statue and trying to understand what all this means. I look around for Harrison, but he's gone. Probably back in the driveway with his basketball. Or downstairs in front of the TV. After a long minute, Mrs. Nanda finds her voice again. "We came to this country for a better life. But my husband questions whether we found one. I know he was unhappy about the way he was treated at his job. He discussed leaving many times. But I never thought ..." She wipes her eyes with the edge of the tissue. "I am very afraid for what this could mean. And I did not know what else to do, so I came here." She turns her eyes back to me now. "I was hoping Pinky might be with you."

"No. She went with Mr. Nanda," I say really slowly 'cause I'm not sure if this is helping or not. But it's the truth, so I have to say it. "I saw his car in front of the school. Pinky was in the backseat. She waved to me."

Turns out it is the wrong thing to say because it makes Mrs. Nanda break into tears all over again. "He has stolen them both. I am sure of it," she wails, covering her face with her hands. Mom leans forward and puts a hand over Mrs. Nanda's shoulder.

I feel bad watching her cry, so I start crying, too. I'm scared for Pinky and Padma. Something awful is happening to them, even though I'm not exactly sure I understand what. Stolen? How can kids be stolen by their own father? After a minute, Mom comes over, hunches down next to me and takes me by the arms. She leans close and looks into my eyes, like there's a message inside them she's trying to read. "Calm down, Finch. I need you to think carefully," she says. She's using her most serious voice — the one she usually only uses when I've done something wrong and she's trying really hard not to blow her lid. "Did Pinky say anything to you that could help? Do you have any idea where she might have gone?"

I push my hand over my eyes, wiping away the mess of spilled tears. My heart is pounding so hard, I think it might fly out of my chest. I'm trying hard to remember anything that Pinky might have said about her father. Anything that could help make this better. Maybe I'm not big enough to quit school and help Terry Fox finish his run. Maybe I'm not smart enough to figure out a way to help those hostages get free. Maybe I can't write for beans. And maybe I'm the only kid on the street who can't ride a bike. And maybe, just maybe, the rest of my feathers won't actually grow in and I won't ever fly. But I think I can help Pinky and Padma get out of trouble. Actually, I know I can. 'Cause it's written right there all over Mom's face.

I think back to what Pinky said in class this morning. And to our conversation in the candy aisle a few days ago.

"She told me her dad wants to take her to India. He told Pinky they'll be going there soon. But not to tell because it's supposed to be a surprise." My voice sounds as thin as a soap bubble.

Mom's eyes widen. She and Mrs. Nanda stare at each other and I get a weird feeling like they're talking even though nobody is saying a word. Before I can ask what's going on, Mom puts her hands on my back and shoos me right out of the kitchen. "Thank you, Finch. Go to your room and wait for me to come get you." She pulls the kitchen door shut behind me before I can even ask what she's going to do.

I want to find Harrison and tell him what's just happened. But I don't want to go where Mom can't find me, in case she needs me to help some more. I take my time going up the stairs, keeping my eyes and ears glued to that kitchen door 'cause I'm still scared and I don't want to miss anything. There's lots of hushed talking and crying coming from behind it. I hear the sound of the faucet running. And the sound of someone dialing the telephone. I hear Mom's voice asking for Daddy's friend Detective Kroon. Mom sounds like she's in a big hurry. I hear her say the word *emergency*. And the word *airport*.

And then a minute later, I hear her say the word *kidnapped*.

CHAPTER 15

I'm still lingering on the stairs when Mom comes out of the kitchen and finds me. She's holding her purse in one hand and her key chain in the other. Her eyes are wet and wild, like hurricanes. "I'm going out for a while," she says, throwing her purse strap over her shoulder. Her lighter drops to the floor, but she's in such a hurry she doesn't even bother picking it up. "Stay here with Harrison," she commands. "Don't leave the house until I come back."

Mrs. Nanda is beside her, twisting on her tissue like she's trying to wring the white out of it. Mom's hands are shaking as she fumbles with the loop of jingling keys. As soon as she finds the one she's looking for, she puts a hand on Mrs. Nanda's arm and they turn to leave. Without a word from either of them to tell me what's happening,

"Wait!" I jump to my feet. "Where are you going?"

"To the airport," Mom calls over her shoulder. "We're going to bring Pinky and her sister back."

She's talking loud and walking like she's in a big hurry. Before I know it, the two of them are out the front door. And I'm flying down the stairs so fast, my feet barely skim the carpet. Pushing on my flip-flops, I race to catch up to them in the driveway. The garage door is open and Mom's unlocking the car. Harrison is standing off to the side, cradling his basketball with one hand and scratching his head with the other.

"I'm coming, too," I gasp, reaching for the car door handle.

Mom glances at me. "No, Finch. I need you to —"

"I'm coming!" I'm practically yelling now, but I don't care. I can't let them leave me behind. Not if there's a chance I can help. "Pinky's my friend. I'm coming," I say again. And before anyone can tell me no, I'm yanking open the back door of the car and strapping on my seat belt.

Mom and Mrs. Nanda get into the front seat. I guess both of them are in way too much of a panic to argue, 'cause nobody says boo to me. Mom revs the engine and charges the car down the driveway, faster than a bull rushing a red flag. Mrs. Nanda is huddled in the seat beside her. She's not crying anymore. But she's not talking either. Her arms are crossed over her chest and the look on her face is like how Mom looked on Daddy's funeral day — like someone's sucked every last drop of life right out of her.

Mom's gripping the steering wheel hard; her hands are a pair of tight fists. "Detective Kroon said he'll meet us at the airport. He told me that British Airways has the only flight to New Delhi today."

"It will probably connect through London," Mrs. Nanda says. She's speaking so quietly, I can barely hear her. "That is how we flew when we came seven years ago ..."

Mom steers the car up a spiraling ramp onto a busy highway. We're going so fast, I can hear the wind whistling over the back windows. And we're zipping in and out between lanes and around other cars. My whole life, I've never seen Mom drive like this. I really want to ask her what else Detective Kroon said on the phone. And what we're going to do when we get to the airport. And if it's really true that Pinky and Padma are being kidnapped. Maybe it's because of the way she's driving, but I feel like I might throw up if I try to talk, so I just sit on my hands and button my lips. I've never been so nervous in my life. It's like a nest of worms has hatched in my stomach and now they're crawling around looking for a way out. The sun through the windshield is hot, but nobody bothers to roll down a window. I'm so nervous, I barely even notice the vinyl seats sticking to my thighs. And that's saying a lot.

"If he gets them to India, he will keep them there," Mrs. Nanda says. "He will take them to his parents' home in Punjab and will not allow them to come back here. Aah ... will I ever see my little daughters again?" Her voice breaks over this last part, and that makes me want to cry, too. I'm so scared for Pinky and her sister. I know how horrible it is to lose a parent. But I can't imagine how it would feel if my other parent made it happen.

"The detective is a good friend of ours. He'll stop your husband in time. Don't worry," Mom says. She takes her right hand off the steering wheel and reaches for Mrs. Nanda's. And in that little moment, it's like they've been friends forever, even though they just met this afternoon. I think about that welcome-to-the-neighborhood casserole Mom never baked and never delivered, and I'm wondering if she's feeling as sorry about that now as I am. "You will get your girls back," she says softly. "You *will*."

Mrs. Nanda doesn't answer. I guess at this point, what is there to say anyway? More than anything, I want Mom to be right — like she's been right about nearly everything my whole life. She has to be right about getting Pinky and Padma back. Because I can't even begin to understand how they might go away forever. How can two little kids be here one day and gone the next?

A few minutes later, the car slows to a crawl, the zipping between lanes comes to a stop, and I hear Mom muttering something under her breath about "damn rush-hour traffic." I don't say a word because Mom seems so focused on getting to the airport, I think she's forgotten I'm even here, and I'm not sure I want to remind her in case she's ready to yell at me about it now. I sit like a statue, skin sticking to the vinyl and eyes flicking between the dashboard clock and the little yellow light that's just come on next to the steering wheel. I know that light means we're close to running out of gas. But neither Mom nor Mrs. Nanda is saying a word about it. Because if we do run out of gas, we'll never make it, and that's way too scary to say out loud. My thoughts flash back to those poor baby birds in the nest and how horrible it felt when I couldn't stop Matt from hurting them. I can't even imagine how much more horrible it would feel if we can't help Mrs. Nanda get Pinky and Padma back. Mrs. Nanda's eyes are closed and her hands are clasped over her heart. I remember the day I saw her praying in front of that little gold statue in her living room. I wonder if she's praying now. I wonder if I should pray, too. The only time I ever tried praying was when Daddy was dying. And it didn't do any good. But I think I'm going to give it a try one more time.

Right now. Just in case.

I close my eyes to pray because that seems to be how it's done. And like I said before, sometimes it's easier to be brave when you don't have to watch what's in front of you. I run my fingertips over my feather scar and think my most powerful thoughts. And maybe this time my prayer does do some good, because when we get off the highway, the traffic is clear and Mom picks up speed again. I know we must be close to the airport now 'cause there are big white planes flying over our heads. The gas light seems to be glowing brighter than ever. But the engine hasn't cut out yet.

"Almost there," Mom says, veering off toward a sign that reads *Airport Road*. I'm so nervous, my head is spinning. Every time she brakes, the engine makes a clunking noise, and I imagine I'm hearing the airplane door closing behind Pinky and Padma. And every time she turns a corner, the tires screech and I imagine I'm hearing my friend crying for her mom. When we finally pull up at the airport, Mom parks the car in front of the British Airways sign and the three of us jump out and run inside. I've never been inside an airport before, so I don't even know where to start looking. But Mom and Mrs. Nanda stop in front of a big black board with lots of numbers on it.

"There!" Mrs. Nanda says, pointing to a row of numbers near the top. "British Airways flight to London. Gate 21. We only have twenty minutes!"

The two of them start running toward the gate, and I follow as fast as I can in my flip-flops. I trip a couple of times but somehow manage to keep up. I'm starting to think we're going to make it, when suddenly the three of us get stopped by a long line of people waiting to walk through a metal detector.

Mom groans, checking her watch. Mrs. Nanda twists her bracelets around and around her thin wrist. She bites her lip as she watches the line slowly inch forward.

"Come on, come on," Mom says, bouncing up and down on her heels like she's ready to take a giant leap over the heads of the people in front of us.

"Are we going to make it on time?" I ask, grabbing on to her arm.

Mom just shrugs and shakes her head. I'm not

sure if that means yes or no, but I don't think I should ask again. I wonder where Detective Kroon is. Didn't he say he'd be here? I stand on my tiptoes, trying to count how many people are in line ahead of us. Just beyond the metal detector, I can see a white sign with black letters pointing down a long hallway. The sign says *To Gates 15–30*.

Gate 21 must be right down there.

Without stopping to think, I duck under someone's elbow and sneak my way up to the front of the line. "Finch!" I hear Mom call out from behind me. But I don't slow down for a second. Before anybody can stop me, I'm slipping through the metal detector. And now I'm tearing down the long hall to Gate 21.

"Finch!"

All I can think about is getting to Pinky and Padma in time. I trip and fall over my flip-flops once more. These stupid shoes aren't meant for running. So I pull them off and run the rest of the way barefoot. As I reach Gate 21, I spot Mr. Nanda standing with the girls. He's handing tickets to a lady in a blue suit. My heart stops.

"Pinky!" I scream, racing ahead.

She doesn't turn around, but Mr. Nanda must have heard me because he glances quickly over his shoulder, then takes each girl by the hand and pulls them toward the mouth of a dark hallway. "Pinky!" I scream again, just as Mom, Mrs. Nanda and Detective Kroon catch up. This time, Pinky stops walking and turns her head. Her big brown eyes connect with mine. And then her mother's. And then she pulls away and dashes toward us. Mr. Nanda calls after her, but Pinky doesn't stop until she's in her mother's arms. She's crying and I'm crying and Mrs. Nanda is holding on to her like she's never going to let her go. There's shouting everywhere, and Mom's arms come around me. I hold on so tight, I'm sure I must be hurting her, but I can't stop myself. And I don't know where they came from, but suddenly there's a swarm of policemen there with us at Gate 21.

My eyes are blurry with tears, but not so blurry that I can't see Detective Kroon carrying a wailing Padma back to her mother. And behind him, I see Mr. Nanda being led away in handcuffs. His eyes connect with mine as he passes. They're teary, too. I turn my face back into the shelter of Mom's arms.

I think I should be angry at him for trying to steal Pinky and Padma away. But I just feel sad.

CHAPTER 16

October 1980

Pinky and Padma's photo got on the front page of the newspaper, just like Terry Fox. There was a big story about them and how they were almost kidnapped by their father. The newspaper mentioned Detective Kroon and even included a small photo of me and some words about how I helped. For a couple of days, I felt famous. All of a sudden, kids who had been ignoring me for almost a year started talking to me again. Just because I was in the newspaper. When Pinky came back to school a few days later, they asked for her autograph. She got so much attention, she was like a movie star. Even awful Matt didn't dare call her another bad name.

A few days after the whole kerfuffle was finished, Mom finally sent me next door with that long-overdue casserole. Mom's been cooking a little bit more lately, which makes me happy. In return, Mrs.

Nanda sent Mom and me and Harrison an invitation to come for tea. This time when I rang their doorbell, Pinky answered right away.

She and Padma don't have their father home with them anymore. Kind of like me, but different. Pinky said she cries about her dad sometimes. She misses him badly, even though she knows he made a big mistake. Her mother's looking for a job, too. And I heard Mom saying she'd help her find one. I'm going to keep my eyes open also. After all, I was the one who found Mom a job, right?

Pinky's still going to school, but Mrs. Nanda walks her there and picks her up every day. I walk with them, and sometimes she's allowed to come over to my house and play in the afternoon. And sometimes I'm allowed to go over there. We make sunbonnets out of T-shirts and play *Little House on the Prairie*, and we pretend we're Mary and Laura, but both of us want to be Laura, so we have to take turns. Sometimes we do homework together. And sometimes she helps me practice my writing and spelling. But we always make it fun so it doesn't feel anything like school.

Last night I woke up and the moon was in my window. It was shining so big, for a second I thought I must be looking at the sun. And so bright, my room lit up like a summer day. It made me feel hot, so I kicked off my quilt and let it drop to the floor.

That's when I noticed them. My feathers. They'd grown in. White and soft and curling over every inch of me like a layer of rabbit fur. I stood up and stretched, and saw that my arms were wings. So I climbed onto my window ledge, pushed out my screen and flew up toward that big bright moon. I flew so far and so fast, I knew I might never find my way back. But that didn't stop me or even slow me down. I flew over a wide black ocean. I flew over a long gray road that stretched across flat land like a ribbon over a box. I flew over a thick forest and through a narrow tunnel, toward a bright light that wasn't the moon or even the sun. And that's where I finally found Daddy.

"Finch," he said, smiling like he knew all along I'd be coming. He looked healthy and strong, just the way he used to look before he got sick. And he had beautiful white wings, too, just like mine. He took my feathered hand in his and we flew together until the big bright moon melted back into the sky. And then he stopped and told me I couldn't fly any farther. "It's time to go, Finch," he said.

I clung to his hand. "No, I want to stay with you, Daddy."

"I can't let you do that," he said softly. "You need to go back to Mom and Harrison. They need you." And he kissed me and told me I'm going to be okay. Then he turned me around and sent me back home.

This morning I'm back in my bed and my feathers are all gone. And I guess it must have been a dream, and I'm sad for a bit. But it makes me think about how Pinky and Padma almost flew away to the other side of the world. And how close I came to never seeing them again. I turn toward the window, run a finger over my scar and think about everything that's happened in the past few weeks. How I got my old mom back. And how I stood up to awful Matt. And how I found a new friend. And how maybe I don't really need the rest of my feathers to grow in, after all.

This afternoon, Mom gets a call from somebody important in the government. I don't remember what his name is or the job he has, but he tells Mom that there's a big meeting happening in a city called The Hague, in Holland. The people at the meeting are talking about how to prevent "international child abduction" (which Mom says is fancy talk for when kids are stolen away from the country they live in by one of their parents). The man from the government saw the article in the newspaper, and he wants me and Pinky to go and tell our story about what almost happened that day at the airport. He says we'll be talking in front of really important people — ones who can help stop the same thing from happening to other kids around the world. Mom and Harrison and Mrs. Nanda and Padma would come, too. And we'd all go on the airplane together.

Mom tells him that she'll talk to me about it and call him back.

"So what do you think, Finch?" she asks after she hangs up the phone. "Holland is a long way away. Do you want to go?"

Of course, I say yes.

I always knew I had it in me to fly.

Author's Note

The Hague Convention on the Civil Aspects of International Child Abduction was created to help return children who have been wrongfully removed from their home country by one of their parents. The proceedings on the convention concluded on October 25, 1980, and entered into force between the member nations on December 1, 1983.

The three original signing nations were Canada, France and Portugal.

Today, over ninety nations are members of the convention.

For more information, go to www.hcch.net.

Acknowledgments

Firstly, I'd like to thank Yasemin Uçar, Yvette Ghione, Lisa Lyons, Semareh Al-Hillal and the rest of the incredible team at Kids Can Press for their passion and dedication to this story.

Many thanks to my awesome band of first readers: Gordon Pape, Shirley Pape, Kim Pape-Green, Samina Akhtar, Mahtab Narsimhan, Helaine Becker, Simone Spiegel, Tova Rich and Christie Harkin. Thanks also to super-agent Sarah Heller for her wisdom and advice.

I'm very grateful to the Canada Council for the Arts and the Ontario Arts Council for their generous support of this project.

And finally, hugs and heartfelt thanks to my sweet family — Jordy, Jonah and Dahlia — for their love, enthusiasm, humor and unabashed honesty. Always and forever!